I0666391

Take Down Journeys

First Edition

Kyle Cicero

Take Down Journeys

First Edition

Published by The Nazca Plains Corporation
Las Vegas, Nevada
2007

ISBN: 978-1-934625-11-8

Published by

The Nazca Plains Corporation ®
4640 Paradise Rd, Suite 141
Las Vegas NV 89109-8000

PUBLISHER'S NOTE
Take Down Journeys is a work of fiction created wholly by *Kyle Cicero's*
imagination. All characters are fictional and any resemblance to any
persons living or deceased is purely by accident. No portion of this
book reflects any real person or events.

Cover Photo, Corwin
Cover Model, Leo
Art Director, Blake Stephens

DEDICATION

This work is dedicated to family and friends and to readers who enjoyed the journey. Finally to Mark Allen J. the eternal 'muse', Sasha M. who makes it fun and, Cyrus K. who rocks the world and my life. Truly love you Cy.

Take Down Journeys

Kyle Cicero

CONTENTS

DE-ALPHA DOGGED

Prologue

As Brad submitted further in each encounter with Teddy, he could feel an ever-increasing desire for more sexual domination by the slightly effeminate younger boy. Brad's cock was always fully erect during their get-togethers. He felt mortified at how he now debased himself whenever they met, but that very embarrassment produced an overwhelming erotic ecstasy for him that he now constantly craved. The handsome hunk found that during each new sexual degradation and indignity inflicted on him by Teddy he lost any urge to resist. Any mental reservations he experienced were subservient to the consuming wants of his engorged and throbbing dick.

Before this, Brad had always prided himself on his strong personality and physical prowess. As the state champion and captain of the school's wrestling team; the six foot two inch, blonde, green-eyed muscular senior had ruled the campus with a breezy arrogant confidence. With his Abercrombie good looks and sculpted body, he easily scored on any girl he wanted and had lorded over every guy with a smug superiority. Now no matter how macho and haughty Brad was with the girls who swooned over and flirted with him, Brad could not forget that Teddy, lisping, swishy, five foot six inch Teddy, had found the way to de-top his self-assured macho sexual persona. Teddy, a nerdy freshman, had taken him down physically and mentally. Brad's knowledge that this skinny book-worm, who openly stated his own desire for feminization and domination from other men, had kicked his athletic butt and sexually cold-conked his heterosexual alpha-dog self-image only increased the hunky senior's own sexual addiction for degradation and submission to Teddy.

The scrawny geek now called the shots and it was the hunky jock that meekly surrendered sexually every time and performed on command to Teddy's every whim. Brad's self-important condescending attitude crumbled under Teddy's taunting domination of the former BMOC.

Brad recalled his conceited statement when Teddy had first

made a pass at him. 'I don't do guys you fag and I'd never bottom for you if I did'. Things had certainly changed. Teddy had bitched the campus' jock hero, had repeatedly abused and bottomed him sexually and worse, Brad actually craving for more!

Looking back now, it all began to unwind for Brad a month ago…

Part One

"Oh yes baby harder please," Sheila gasped as Brad pumped his thick 9-inch cock deep inside her slippery hole. Brad grinned to himself as his hefty low hangers slapped her flesh. He loved that feeling he got as his nuts swayed.

"Yeah," he thought as he increased his strokes, "take it bitch. Take my fucking meat." He enjoyed it when the girls begged him to do it to them. He visualized his powerfully sculpted body ramming into them. He was a stud, he thought, definitely a babe magnet. His thoughts suddenly recalled the day's events. In particular, a skinny slight faggot named Teddy who had the nerve to make a pass at him in the in study hall. Had even suggested he, the star of the school, might like taking it up his shitter!

"Fuck," he growled as he thrust harder, remembering the incident. Sheila thinking it was she that caused his reply just smiled and held on to his tapered waist with her legs.

"He had a fucking nerve thinking I was a faggot like him," Brad silently reflected. "And he even had the nerve to comment on how hot my ass would be and that he would be home alone tonight if I wanted to get 'stuffed'. If that teacher hadn't been there that puny pussy would be dead meat." Brad's temper rose and he increased his screwing. Sheila was moaning in heat as Brad's pumped faster. "Me, his fucking faggot? As if that muther could plow my butt!" He climaxed still enraged. "That faggot needs to be shown who rules!" Brad decided. He pulled out.

"Hmmm baby," Sheila cooed as she ran her hands across his hard body. "You were hot just then."

Brad wasn't even paying attention. He was now riled by Teddy's actions. "Got to go babe." He said as he pulled on his sweats.

"WHAT!" Sheila gasped in surprise.

"Got business from today to finish," He replied as he left. Brad decided to take Teddy up on his offer of a visit. "We'll see who gets fucked up the ass tonight," he muttered as he rushed out. If Brad only knew how true, his words were!

A Boner Book

Part Two

Teddy saw Brad pull up. He smirked to himself. "Yeah I knew making that pass would get you here," he said softly to the empty room. Teddy had been planning this for a while. His father a noted chemist and addiction counselor was away on another routine conference with his mom. Teddy as his only child had learned quite a lot from his dad about drugs, addiction, and the workings of the brain. Today he was going to use it all to 'pin' that smug sexy wrestler that he had lusted after since he first saw him. He heard Brad pounding on the door. Teddy had prepared a special room that only he had a key for. Tonight he was going to use it, as well as its contents. He went to let his victim in!

Brad pushed his way in once the door opened. He turned to face Teddy and grabbed his shirt. "We got issues you faggot we need to settle," he muttered as he leaned in close. "I'm going to fuck you bad you pathetic queen."

Teddy stayed calm. "Sure, okay. But my mom is upstairs sick. Can we go to my room downstairs?" He replied feigning fear. "I swear I won't try anything."

Brad smirked. "Fine you fag. But don't think getting me alone in your room will get you any closer to getting in my ass. One bad move and I'll pound your to dust okay." Brad saw he'd scared the shit out of the twerp and the thought of that limp wristed punk could ever take him almost caused him to break out laughing. "Yeah you trying to take me on that's a laugh alright. But one move and..."

"Yes I understand." Teddy said as he took Brad downstairs. He opened the door and let Brad saunter through ahead of him. Brad saw that the room was only furnished with some type of electric machine by a table with bottles on it. He turned to face Teddy.

"What kind of place is," the hunky jock never finished as Teddy pulled out a bottle and sprayed something full force into Brad's face. "WHAT THE FUCK." Brad managed to reply before the burning hit his eyes. "YOU FUCKER," Brad roared as he tried to blindly reach out and grab where he thought Teddy was. "I'll FUCKING TAKE YOU APART!"

Teddy however had quickly moved behind the powerful wrestler who flailed his arms about wildly trying to find and beat his opponent. Teddy grabbed Brad around the neck from behind and put him in a chokehold. Holding on tight and literally leaping onto Brad's strong back he started to cut off Brad's oxygen.

"GET THE FUCK OFF ME." Brad screamed as he tried to throw Teddy off his back. Teddy gripped tighter. Brad soon discovered that not only was he sightless, he was rapidly losing his airflow. "GET OFF OF ME YOU FAGGOT!" Brad cursed as his intake of oxygen diminished. He started to feel the first effects as his consciousness decreased.

"Going beddy bye stud," Teddy laughed mockingly as he cinched in tighter. The thrill of imminent victory aroused Teddy now.

"NO WAY I'M GOING OUT," Brad howled as he flexed and struggled. No way was this puny younger faggot going to take this star athlete down, especially with a wrestling move his mind yelled. He bellowed and gyrated in vain as Teddy, now enjoying the ride on his muscular stallion, held onto him fast, and squeezed his grip further. Teddy could feel the powerful definition of the jock that writhed under him. If Brad hadn't been otherwise occupied, he would have discerned that Teddy had thrown an impressive boner that rubbed maliciously between the strong back muscles of the increasingly weakening wrestler.

"Go to sleep bro," Teddy smirked as he felt Brad's efforts flagging. Teddy was ecstatic. He was taking down the campus hero. He recalled Brad's strutting demeanor in the past. His boast to his fellow wrestlers that HE never went down. Well if they could only see it, he thought. "I'm beating you!" He said sharply. "I'm taking you and I'm putting you out!"

Brad couldn't! He wouldn't let some lisping queen take him.

"NO... WAY," Brad croaked as he felt the room spin. He flailed his arms wildly but the strapping stud felt his knees buckle, his resistance lost momentum, and his muscular arms soon flopped limply to his sides. "Never...beaten," he muttered quietly.

"That's right go to sleep," Teddy cooed to his victim. "Big jock boy going down tonight huh." The younger boy could sense his victory was almost there. He lewdly rubbed his throbbing dick between Brad's back muscles. "You're getting beat bro." He hooted in delight.

"No...fuc...wwaaaooooowww," Brad panted. Brad felt Teddy lowering him to the ground as his breathing softened into a slow rhythmic pattern. His hard butt hit the ground, "oooofffff," Brad grunted as he expelled more air. His tapered legs spread out in a 'V' infront of him. He couldn't rise and his arms got heavy. Brad fell back against Teddy as the scrawny boy finished him off. Brad tried to raise one muscled arm to swat Teddy but lost it half way up. The arm fell back down and his hand rested in his lap. "Nooott…gooinngg…unnndderrrr," he quietly whispered as he lost it.

"Sleepy time bro," cooed Teddy. "That's right sleepy time." He could feel the hard muscles of his opponent going limp and pressing against him. "Nap time stud." He increased his grip and pulled back so Brad was supported by Teddy's embrace. "Sleepy time."

Brad mumbled incoherently in reply. "Uuuummuuhh." His chest rising and falling as he went under farther, "nooooottt… sleeeeeeppyyyy."

"Putting you out hot-shot," Teddy whispered to Brad gleefully as he cradled a fast drifting jock into a nice nap. "That's right cutie go to sleep for Teddy."

"Ummmmmmmm," just before Brad lost consciousness a final shocking thought exploded his mind: Teddy, small geeky effeminate Teddy had taken him down. "Noooooooooooooo," Brad rasped as the lights went out. His hot body went fully slack while a tiny bit of saliva dripped from his mouth. Teddy held on a bit more watching the shallow rise and fall of Brad's chest and stomach. He reached over to lift one of Brad's arms and watched as it dropped like a dead weight.

"Yep you're out cutie," Teddy chuckled as he released his grip and pushed the hunk off him. Brad slumped sideways to the ground. He looked so peaceful and sexy.

Teddy smiled at the crumpled body lying before him. He quickly pulled off Brad's sweats taking just enough time to admire his strong firm body. Brad was chiseled perfection and his basket was impressive. What Teddy really loved was the wrestlers hot bubble ass. Teddy felt his own rod stiffen once more but he realized he had to get on with business. Eagerly he lifted the unconscious stud onto the table and tied him down. He reached over and attached wires from the machine to various spots on Brads head. Each spot was located over an addiction center in the knocked-out athlete's brain. Teddy knew that through the use of electrical stimuli he could activate an addiction response in Brad. Given sufficient time, he could cause the young jock to become an addict to whatever he was experiencing while the stimulus was turned on. Teddy carefully wired some sexual spots on his jock and injected a strong psychotropic drug into Brad. Teddy wanted to be sure that his victim's mental processes were screwed up enough to help the progression and that Brad got some outside sexual incentive in certain places. Thanks to his chemical knowledge, he was able to lace it with a powerful sexual stimulant. He grazed the back of his hand across Brad's cheek. "Big shot." He growled. "Strutting around. Showing off. So cock-sure. Speaking of which." Teddy let his hands run along Brad's sculpted torso resting at last on Brad's thick cock. Teddy gently began to stroke knocked-out stud's meat causing it to slightly rise.

"Ohhhh," Brad sighed as a look of contentment came to his handsome face. His rod stiffened and his low hangers rose up a bit.

"Thought what the fuck, he's a screaming queen." Teddy said roughly, as he teased Brad's meat to a full erection. "Going to fuck me over huh? Maybe, with this, you arrogant macho jackass. Well bud this is one queen that likes to fuck. And after I'm done with you it's going to be you that prefers getting fucked!" The room filled with Teddy's laughter as he continued fondling the helpless wrestling star who mumbled as if in agreement. "Yeah this is one queer that knows how to turn a straight bull like you into a docile sissified heifer! Any objections ass-hole?"

Brad just lay there silently with a goofy relaxed smile on his handsome face.

Part Three

It went on for hours as Teddy methodically went about his plan. Brad's drug addled brain was subjected to a continuous whirl of experiences. Shame, feelings of degradation, helpless inability to resist, and through it all, a series of overarching erotic thrills that went beyond any he had experienced with women. The formerly arrogant sports star learned to appreciate a completely new sexual menu.

"No …I can't," Brad begged, as Teddy demanded the campus hero rim him that initial time.

"Well, I won't force you to but..." Teddy slyly replied as he lightly stroked Brad's engorged cock. "But, if you do I'll jerk you off as you do it. In fact, the better you do it, the more I'll...well?" Teddy just smiled and increased the electrical vibrations to Brad's body and brain. The young athlete's rod vibrated and thickened as its head reddened. He felt Teddy's fingers and longed for more of that hand to grip his cock, and give him relief. Teddy flicked at Brad's dick coyly teasing. Could Brad hold out?

Sweat poured out of Brad's tormented body. Eat out a guy's ass. Brad was disgusted at the perverse idea. "Fuck you…fuck you …you faggot." He screamed. Teddy just laughed. As his body went into a frenzy of arousal, he began to crack up. He felt Teddy's fingers gently run down the underside of his shaft. His body shivered at how good it felt. "OH GOD I NEED TO CUM," Brad screamed, "OKAY. OKAY!"

Teddy nearly shouted in joy. He straddled Brad's head, lowered his butt onto that handsome face, and felt the tentative moist touch of Brad's tongue as he ate his first chute.

"Lick it bro," Teddy sighed, "lick it out good and I swear I'll beat you off." True to his word, Teddy reached down and stroked Brad's meat and reveled as the young stud licked away in a frenzy timed with the quickened masturbation he was getting from Teddy.

Brad was repulsed, yet his sexual hunger was satisfied. The young hunk tongued out Teddy's ass in a sort of semi-delirious state. He kept thinking how deprived he was but the need to be sexually serviced was too strong to resist. He slobbered and washed out that butt knowing that by doing so Teddy was giving him what he had to have. In fact, the waves of lust that Teddy was calming only increased his efforts in rimming. He tasted the folded flesh around Teddy's hole, and then his tongue went beyond to the inner tube. To Brad's surprise it was soft and satiny. He heard Teddy moan and he felt the younger boy quicken his hand job on his cock. His mind realized what he was doing. He experienced a wave of embarrassment then a searing sexual heat inside his gut.

His addiction centers logged in both the degradation, sensation, and the erotic relief. The twin emotions were becoming intertwined in that center.

"You roooo…aaaaaa…ck bitch," Teddy gasped as Brad felt a splash of hot liquid hit his six-pack. Teddy had cum. Brad lost it and climaxed. Brad's muffled grunts when he shot were music to Teddy's ears. When Teddy finally lifted his ass from off the handsome athlete's face, he gleefully observed that amazed, yet contented look in Brad's eyes. "We only have just begun bro." Teddy said quietly. He knew a barrier had been breached. The BMOC superstar had eaten out a guy's butt, cum while he did it and, even better, Brad knew all this. The next time would be easier.

"Hey Braddie not bad. You're a natural ass-eater boy." Teddy teased. "Let's see how you suck dick okay!" Brad's eyes dully focused on the younger geek. He said nothing, but his blue eyes filling with tears spoke volumes. "I think you are still hungry though," Teddy joked as he injected Brad with more of the drug and re-lowered his wet hole onto Brad's face. Grabbing the rod in front of him and turning the current slightly higher, Teddy enjoyed a second rim job. "Yeah, sucking cock, but first I'll think of some other sex acts," Teddy mused. "After all, we got all night!"

And so it went for Brad. No matter how nauseated he was by the other sexual acts required of him, his drug induced, overpowering lusts always got the better of him. With each humiliating sexual deed he performed or let be performed on him Teddy permitted, Brad's to 'get off'. Electrically placed patches on Brad's erogenous zones and on his skull stimulated his pleasure centers while encouraging his addiction centers into overdrive. He soon discovered a gnawing desire growing for more of the experiences. A sort of fundamental need was coming to life in him that crushed any former hostility; reluctance to what was happening, or what he was doing. He was subjected to a series of sexual situations that filled him with disgust, yet he was also in a state of continuous erotic arousals of a kind he'd never been in before and, to his embarrassment, he still wanted more! If he had been in a clear state of mind, he might have realized that the addiction/pleasure centers in his brain were now completely overdosed thanks to the bolts of vibrating electrical currents that Teddy was inducing to him, and that the arousals were merely drug and electrically produced. But in his chemically disorientated mental state, Brad was incapable of any such rationalizations. Teddy however was well aware that Brad's disgust and shame only aided in the process by releasing powerful emotions that could be tapped and redirected to Teddy's own ends. It wasn't enough for him to sexually conquer Brad. He wanted the smug jock to hate what he would be compelled by his created 'addiction' to do. Both sensations were being written in tandem in Brad's brain to that end.

"That's right open wide," Teddy encouraged as he flicked his cock across Brad's full lips. Teddy rested comfortably on the young athlete's six-pack. He enjoyed the sensation of them on his bare butt. Teddy reached behind and made sure that he had a grip on Brad's manhood, which was getting a nice stroke to full flower. "Open up and suck my cock buddy."

"No...please...I...I...not that," Brad shivered even as his raging hormones screamed out to do it to get off.

"I'll let you cum again." Teddy snickered as he enjoyed seeing the conflict play out on Brad's handsome face. He increased his hand job on Brad's rod.

"Don't...please...not sucking dick," Brad pleaded to Teddy's delight. Teddy increased his masturbation on the hunk. Brad's brain spun and his resistance began to crack up. "Suck your dick...I...I"

"Do it. You want to. Need to. Get off. Get off. Get off," Teddy chanted in a rhythmic monotone while he ran the palm of his other hand across Brad's sculpted pectorals and tweaked Brad's nipples to rock hard bullets. Brad needed to suck voluntarily and Teddy was patient. He rested his cock-head on Brad's trembling lower lip. The pre-cum ran across Brad's full lips and into Brad's throat.

The salty fluid made its way down the back of the hunk's throat, which caused Brad to involuntarily swallow. The prone wrestler immediately realized he had just tasted a man's spunk. He wanted to die of shame. Little did he realize that very emotional response would defeat his resistance. The addictions center felt it and its twin colleague of desire flared up. Brad whimpered pathetically as his cock demanded action now. He began to cry and his mouth opened. His tongue tentatively lapped the head of Teddy's cock.

"Good boy," encouraged Teddy as he let Brad set the pace. He stroked and watched as Brad's eyes glazed. He was turning Brad on again. The wrestling star licked more of the head in front of him. A few more manipulations on Brad's cock set the deal. Brad's mouth opened wider, and Teddy slipped in.

Brad's eyes popped open "Uuuuummpphh," came out as a muffled sound. Teddy pulled out letting Brad suck in air. "CCCCaaaaaaa," Brad coughed, "I don't think I can," but Teddy cut him off.

"Relax. Just get it wetter and you'll see," he cooed as he massaged Brad's rod. Brad groaned with lust and started to bathe the hard dick with his saliva. With patient instruction from Teddy, the feverish jock learned the fine art of sucking cock. Teddy plunged his meat back in brad's throat.

"Uuuuummphh," Brad mumbled as he sucked. His good-looking visage was distorted by a mouth full of dick. Teddy smiled and beat Brad's meat. Brad's tongue worked on the dick that was now deep in his throat.

"If they could see their big hero sucking my cock," he chuckled loudly as Brad, now totally humiliated, felt that all too familiar rush of erotic arousal that came with such emotions. "We are just starting our treatments," Teddy thought as he plowed Brad's hot moist mouth. Brad, now helplessly turned on by his addiction centers, continued licking and lapping on the hard object in his mouth. His nose filled with Teddy's sexual scent, and his chin felt the constant slapping of Teddy's balls. To his shame he shot a wad high in the air. "Yes," Teddy nodded to himself. "We are on a roll!"

By the conclusion of Teddy's 'initial' treatments, it was over for the handsome strapping campus hero. Brad accepted inside himself that it was imperative to satisfy the 'need' that burned in him, and he now assumed that it was these desires coupled with the intense degradation he felt as they occurred were the only way to accomplish it. In fact, in his drugged and disorientated brain, it seemed that it was the latter, which made the former even hotter. The more he hated, the more he despised, the greater the sexual thrill which, once sated, momentarily stilled that ravenous craving. It was apparent that he required both emotional kindling's to feed the howling demands that literally burned inside him tonight. His confused mental centers were engaged in a sort of recalculating: overwhelming sexual thrill plus undeniable personal humiliations together equals necessary satisfaction. It would take time to fully process the math, set it permanently into his brain, and fundamentally alter Brad's sexuality, but for now the hot stud reluctantly reasoned to himself that he had to slake this relentless appetite to do what was necessary to debase himself. As this realization hit home, his self-image as a powerful, athletic, unconquerable, super-stud collapsed. "Fuck I need more again." He groaned at one point after having sucked Teddy's meat and sack for what seemed like the sixth time. As usual during the endeavor, he had climaxed. As typical, the twin emotions of longing and mortification locked into his addictive centers.

"Pardon," Teddy teased as he reached over to turn up the electrical stimuli. Brad twitched as Teddy massaged the bound hunk's cock once more. Brads impressive rod rose to full staff causing the muscular jock to twitch for more sexual release.

It was all over, Brad decided the effeminate nerd had finally won. The unconquerable macho jock had been taken down by someone he had previously considered physically weaker and contemptuous. Now for the hardest part, telling this frail gay wuss that he had not only whupped Brad's straight butt but that Brad longed to be fucked over by him again. He pathetically began to verbalize his humiliating loss. It was at that moment Teddy heard the next words that sent him in rapture.

"I give." Brad mumbled hesitantly. "More please,"

"What was that?" Teddy queried in hopeful anticipation.

The tall powerful hunk cringed upon hearing Teddy's lisping voice. He yearned for more submission to Teddy and the burning ignominy of that fact all only made him hotter as the 'hunger' flared up in force.

"More…I want more…please," Brad said audibly a broken jock-stud.

"More what?" Teddy quizzed happily. This was a moment meant to be savored and Brad needed to be totally mind fucked by an out-loud admission of his desires from Teddy.

"Need to get off again. Need… I…" Brad whined his voice cracking like a kid as he pled. As he spoke, his rod continued throbbing in heat. "I…please!"

"Go on," Teddy laughed as he watched the formerly arrogant athlete twitching in heat. "What do you want me to do?"

Through bleary hazed eyes, Brad could see his tormentor's smiling face mocking him. He struggled to say it. To admit what he wanted sexually from the smaller frailer boy. The more he felt that despair the more he had to get off and get off in the way he believed would do it. He groaned and said it. "Fucking break me in more...punk my jock assss...pleaseeeeee...getsss...meeee...hotterrrrr,"

"Hmmm. You want me to... fuck you?" Teddy quizzed happily. The final seal on the deal he thought. Getting that arrogant jock to consent to getting his virginal chute plugged.

A crushed Brad lifted his head. The thought of his getting butt-fucked disgusted him. It would be the final indignity. He couldn't permit or want to get his ass fucked. Only wimps, faggots, and girls took it up the rear. Brad was no pussy. His entire being cringed and he felt a surge of uncontrollable mortification as he visualized it being done to him. His brain further processed that emotion and it reinvigorated the correlated sexual desire in him to new heights. Brad's dick was in agony to get relief. He knew the ache had to be satiated anew. He sighed and just gave up. "Fuck yes." He sobbed. He was going to let that effeminate, scrawny geek, fuck away his last shred of manhood.

"Then ask me nicely now," Teddy said haughtily.

"Please," Brad croaked his voice breaking now, "please... fuck...me!"

"Fucking A," Teddy hooted as he ratcheted up the current, gave his hunk a large drug dose, and hoisted Brad's muscular legs apart, preparing to ride his formerly bucking bronco in his own personal rodeo! Little, young, rail thin Teddy had beaten his smug hunky foe and was going to do the unthinkable. Turn hotshot Brad, the school BMOC from a raging alpha male, into a bottom-boy cum dump. "Going to fuck you boy but only cause you asked." He hooted. Brad had asked for it and they both knew it.

"Ooooooooooooooooo mannn," Brad howled in response as Teddy lifted him up so that Brad was now resting solely on his broad shoulders. Teddy pushed against Brad's outer ring. "I...too tight," Brad moaned through gritted teeth. "You're too big!"

"Just let me do it to you. God your worse than a little girl." Teddy knew verbally abusing Brad at this point would turn him on enough to give it up. "Big tough wrestler. Yeah sure." He saw the look of surrender in those blue eyes and Teddy felt Brad's ass muscles loosen.

"OH GOD," Brad was now over the edge. His hole's barriers gave way in a fiery blaze. Suddenly, Teddy was in. The younger boy began to screw the former BMOC. "You're fucking my ass." Brad choked out tearfully. "Oh man you are really fucking my ass," Brad garbled in agony. After a few more thrusts, however Brad's muscles eased up and his formerly virginal chute sucked in its invader as waves of sexual pleasure engulfed him again. His ass was on fire but in a warm enveloping way, and with it came the stirrings of peaceful relief that only came when he shot his jis. Teddy humped into him harder and yet Brad discovered he wanted more. There was a spot Teddy was just about hitting. Each flick by it aroused him to another level. Brad realized that he wanted that spot slapped by Teddy's rod.

Teddy noticed that Brad's hips moved under him. It was as if Brad was humping back. "Oh bro, you're enjoying it aren't you macho boy?"

Brad gazed at Teddy's face with a look of despair and desire. "Fuck me deeper." The stud blushed even as he begged to the amusement of the younger boy. Big bad assed Brad the humpy sculpted wrestler who got all the girls was getting pinned by a physically weaker opponent and loving it! "Hitting a spot." He whispered sheepishly, "feels so good."

"Fantastic," Teddy exclaimed as he went wild ramming in and out of Brad's chute pounding away in joy. "Fucking taking your jock cherry you bitch," he sneered. "Fucking your sweet tight ass. And you're fucking love it!" his words turned Brad's sexual needs into overdrive.

"AAAARGHHHHH YEAHHHHHHHHHHHHHHHH!" Brad howled in agreement, as Teddy worked on Brad's spot and sent the jock into a stratosphere of delight. He began to thrust his hips back harder onto Teddy's cock, and soon he knew from the inside rumbles of his own dick that he was getting ready to explode. "GOING TO CUM...I'm GOING TO...OH SHIT MAN... YOU'RE FUCKING MY JIS OUT OF ME!" He babbled in ecstasy. Hearing that did it for Teddy as well. Both climaxed in tandem. It was the best relief of the night for Brad. Then the realization of it all hit him. He had begged to be fucked and came like a whore while it occurred. He opened his mouth to scream out some sort of denial but was shocked to hear himself whisper hoarsely, "Fuck me again please!"

"Thought you would want more bitch." Teddy smiled as he moved back into position, inserted his meat deep inside, and struck that spot Brad had discovered within his chute. "Guess all that strutting you were doing in school was a cover for you really wanting some dude to fuck your hot bubble butt, huh?"

Brad nodded weakly as his dick's demands took command

once more. Far from protesting the series of anal assaults that followed however, the handsome hunk spent the rest of the night yelling out lewd encouragements to his conqueror. The room was alive with the sights, sounds, and smells of their rutting!

Part Four

Brad left Teddy's bruised, tired, and mentally shocked. His mind spun with flashes of what had happened to him and how he had behaved. That night he went to his room to figure out how to get even with the younger boy. Brad had decided that his conduct, his new found desires were just a fluke. If he took some type of revenge then Teddy would have no hold on him. His life would go back to the way it was. The handsome jock lay on his bed and recalled all that had been done to him. His breathing quickened as his brain replayed the events. The young hunk felt his whole body tingling and he broke out into a cold sweat. As the actions recreated themselves in his mind, Brad's found himself emotionally reliving his experience. It wasn't until he heard himself moaning that he realized he had unconsciously reached down and was stoking himself to arousal. He was shocked to think that he was getting off on thoughts of his humiliation and yet, he found he couldn't resist his actions. He felt a roar of desire engulf him driving a confusing sexual urge to its natural climax. "Ooooooooooooohhhhhhh yyyeahh." He bellowed as he shot his wad, only to restart the process once more.

Afterwards he lay silently in the dark, his face streaked with tears. While he couldn't comprehend, what was going on in his mind one thing was clear. Brad had continuously masturbated to the remembrances of his sexual degradation. And he had enjoyed doing it!

The rest of that week, Brad tried to blot it all out and resume his old life but at night in the quiet of his room the same scene played out for him. He'd want revenge; he'd recall what was done to him and then, his ultimate surrender to the erotic thrill of the memories, which compelled him pump himself into exhaustion. By the weekend, his ravenous sexual desires required him to admit to himself that he needed more than mental pictures. Shaking with longing and loathing, he reached over from his bed to the phone on his nightstand and placed a call he dreaded making but was forced to do by the commands of his throbbing dick. With each ring, he inwardly winced even while his lust increased.

"Hello Teddy," Brad meekly said when he reached the young freshman at home. He knew what he was going to say and could visualize Teddy's grin at his victory. The thought of himself groveling to the scrawny wimp on the other end killed him but also caused his cock to stir impatiently.

"Yes and what can I do for you," Teddy replied sarcastically. He knew he had the bastard!

"Listen... I...ahh...well...I," the once arrogant jock stuttered as he tried to say it out loud and yet still maintain a shred of his old dignity. He looked at himself in the nearby mirror. His taunt muscular body glistening in sweat. He saw his cock rigid and pulsating. As he looked at his face, he saw not the image of a handsome, arrogant, smug jock star but a pathetic beaten pussy! "I was wondering...I mean...if you are ...free," he croaked hoarsely.

"My dad is away again this week. Get your ass over now. Got it!" Teddy barked as he took control of the situation.

"Yes," mumbled Brad in a tone that signaled his resignation.

"Good boy," Teddy answered making sure to emphasis the later word to his conquered hunk.

Brad squirmed as he heard that term yet his cock roared its agreement with delight in hearing it. "And boy," Teddy continued, "If you want me to train you then you better show some respect when you address me. GOT IT!"

"Yes...sir," Brad whined as he unconsciously reached down to rub his crotch area. "A pussy. I'm his fucking pussy," Brad moaned silently to himself as he hung up. The former macho wrestler let that thought pound in his mind while he proceeded to beat his meat. "Pussy," he gasped as he blew a wad that splashed onto his mirror. He showered and slipped off to his training.

That night began a series of nocturnal visits to Teddy. On that first night, Brad's need for sexual release overcame his initial reservations, and he docilely allowed the geeky freshman to re-hook him to the electrical device and ingest whatever drug Teddy commanded. With each subsequent encounter the young hunk's desires grew while his resistance to the machine and drugs diminished. By the end of the week, thanks to the multiple stimulations which increased his addiction response and enflamed Brad's sex drive; the smug, muscular, wrestling star's body and mind were thoroughly obsessed with the pleasures of domination by the slightly younger Teddy. The training continued every night after that with Brad slipping out of his house and into Teddy's 'special room'. Every night Brad succumbed and allowed his powerful physique to be bound to the table in that room and his muscular frame connected and injected. Teddy never failed to feel a renewed thrill at his conquest of the physically more imposing jock. Watching as the muscular stud wimped and obeyed made life a joy. Teddy never got over the charge of observing Brad slowly strip and climb onto the table. Brad's face was a study in shame and desire that the younger dominator continually used to reassert his control. He had punked the campus BMOC! As Brad lay in all his athletic glory stretched out, tied for Teddy's pleasure the lanky younger boy remembered how proud and haughty Brad had been in his athletic ability, and striking good looks. Now he lay prone and squirming in sexual heat for Teddy to command. If the girls could see their sex stud now he thought as Teddy twisted Brad's brown nipples causing a low guttural moan of pleasure from the handsome jock while they hardened. "Got you, you fucking bastard. Got you moaning like a whore for more huh?"

Brad lifted his head slightly and tried to focus on his dominator, "Yessssss," he hissed as his head fell back on the table. He could hear a chuckle from the geeky freshman; he ran his hands across Brad's smoothly defined chest and abs. "Wonder what the young ladies would say seeing you like this! Shall we see how you like getting your holes filled again?"

Brad knew he was too far gone to object to anything Teddy wanted to do to him. His days as a ladies man were over and he knew it. "Fuckkkk me please sir," he groaning through chattering teeth.

Toward the end of the first month, Teddy began to dress Brad in female underwear to further degrade his sexual captive. With the regulation of the drug administered coupled with carefully heighten electrical stimuli during each training session Teddy was able to ensure that Brad would experience ever increasing arousal even as he felt personal contempt for his submission to such dress.

After a month of such reorientation, Brad needed humiliation and degradation to enjoy sex fully. With a sort of perverse pleasure, Teddy lately had insisted that Brad wear pink lace underwear all the time now. Brad complied even as he moaned in protest. Teddy noted however that his stunning captive was sporting an impressive denial of that protest when Teddy first suggested it.

In school, at practice, even in meets it was all Brad could do to suppress an embarrassing arousal as the satin thongs and frilly undergarments sensually rubbed his dick and reminded him of his new status as Teddy's 'bitch'. Surprisingly Brad never wrestled better. On the mat, he rocked with a record pin record that had many talking potential Olympic gold. His athletic prowess had given rise to him acquiring a huge fan base; quite a few whom secretly lusted over the stunning hunk who seemed to epitomize masculine virility. If they only knew that after every meet, the handsome jock raced over to meet with a puny effeminate guy so he could grovel on all fours and submissively lick that geek's nut-sack while that self same puny geek derided the all-American male's athletic achievements they might have rethought their opinions. Teddy knew that Brad's victories were inspired by thus type of reward. Brad savored degradation and his victories on the mat and the praise he received from others after them only made his subsequent humiliation by Teddy hotter for him.

"Such a big man huh," laughed Teddy while Brad sucked and lapped on the balls and cock provided. "Tell me hot-shot, if you are such a big 'man' why are you here licking my crotch clean boy," he taunted. Brad looked up, his mouth filled with Teddy's sack, a small groan of despair came from his lips, but he feverishly continued slurping away! Teddy reached down and tousled the golden haired hunk's head. "Never mind boy we know why," he chuckled as the docile athlete continued his oral service. Teddy's foot flicked Brad's nuts so that they swayed lewdly to and fro. Teddy knew it made Brad hornier when it happened and judging by the athlete's quicker oral service, he wasn't wrong.

In a final 'graduation ceremony' Teddy strapped Brad to a table in the room. The slight freshman hooked up his muscular jock to the machine and injected the stud with a massive dose of the drug. Teddy hit full power and gleefully watched as the once haughty athletic hunk's rod rose to full majesty. While Brad squirmed and begged to shoot Teddy leaned down and whispered into Brad's ear, "Fucking cunt. That's what you are boy. My fucking pussy cunt!" He squeezed Brad's hefty nuts.

"YOU'RE PUSSY CUNT!" Brad howled in agreement, as his rod shot an arch of white cream that spattered onto his chest. Teddy dipped his fingers in the sticky jism and lets Brad lick his fingers clean. Teddy savored his triumph as Brad lapped up his own spunk!

Epilogue

The former BMOC was on all fours in the darkened room. He was naked except for the frilly girly underwear he had just brought to please Teddy. He had gone to a store Teddy directed him too and done what Teddy had required of him. It was run by two old men who were real queens. Brad blushed with embarrassment as he recalled their faces when he introduced himself as a customer and how the men held the lacy undergarments up to Brad's young body to check size. The lewd smile that came to their wrinkled lips when Brad, as Teddy instructed, asked for their help in the back room in trying them on. Brad flushed with shame as he recalled being in the fitting area with the two effeminate men while he modeled a series of frilly pink panties for their approval and later the wheezing grunts as the older men fucked Brad both orally and anally in that back room with their withered cocks. Throughout it, all his own cock had remained erect and he even climaxed, as he was butt-fucked. As he remembered it all once more, he could feel his rod grow and rub sensually against the satiny feel of the panties he wore. Suddenly he heard the familiar clicking of steps down the stairs. Teddy was coming. His breathing increased and beads of sweat dripped down his sculpted pecs and off his six-pack. Brad knew that before the night was over he would experience more sexual degradations and domination. He wanted to get up and run but his raging hard on held him in check.

"My, my," Teddy lisped as he approached taking in the powerful sexy body that was his to command. He gazed at the hard biceps, muscled legs, tapered waist and firm butt cheeks (contained in the frilly underwear Brad was wearing) that he would soon abuse. "Don't we look so pretty in our panties? I think perhaps you should go back to buy some seamed stockings and garters; then maybe we will tape you modeling them." Brad lifted his handsome face. His blue eyes met Teddy's who could see in them a look of shame, yearning submission. "Possibly I'll send copies to your teammates and your dad. Wouldn't that be fun boy?"

Brad let out a low whimper and shuddered even as a wet spot grew in his lacy covered crotch at the thought of it. He was totally aroused by the idea. It humiliated him and thrilled him in equal measure.

"Hmm," Teddy mused. "You know I think I'll put an ad in our local gay paper too. I could use some extra cash. I think it will read: *Formerly smug, arrogant, athletic straight boy looking to be sexually used and abused by men. A true bottom slut who now needs a lot of men to punk him! Thoughts of humiliation, groveling, and denigration get him very hot!*" Brad let out a whine to try to protest but Teddy saw that the young jock's cock was now straining in its satin confinement. The wet spot grew larger. Teddy laughed as he swatted Brad's rump with a quick series of hard strokes.

WHACK

WHACK

WHACK

WHACK

"Ohhhh," Brad grunted as each hit connected. He felt a familiar fiery heat on his cheeks. His mind recalled the first time he had been spanked by Teddy. How he had meekly crawled over Teddy's lap after unsuccessfully pleading with the younger tormentor not to make him do this; how he had felt as Teddy lowered his CK's; the way Teddy had rubbed his hands across Brad's smooth mounds; the cool air that he felt on them just before that initial slap that began the series of hits that tanned his butt for the first time in his life. He still shuddered with a mix of ignominy and excitement as he remembered how he had bawled like a baby in the end. But most of all he recollected how, throughout every step of it, his cock had stayed rigid. Brad's cock throbbed as he contemplated that ultimate display of his powerlessness. The wet spot grew larger still. "Ugh. Ugh. Ugh. You're whipping my ass again." He groaned.

Teddy stopped then smirked as he pulled out his dick. He strolled around and went up to Brad. "Going to whip your butt again tonight. Got anything to say about that boy?"

Brad, the once frisky stallion now thoroughly gelded, merely parted his sensual lips so Teddy's could insert his dick. As Brad's ears filled with his slurping sounds, the punked athlete knew the evening was just beginning and blissful future degradations awaited him. "MMMMMMMMMMMMM," Brad gulped as Teddy shot a load down his throat. As Teddy laughed, Brad came.

DE-ALPHA DOGGED: TEDDY'S SUMMER ADVENTURE

Part One:
It Begins

Teddy looked around the ranch. The heat and dust of the place were depressing as hell and he inwardly cursed his father's decision to send him to visit his uncle at his ranch out west for the summer. Teddy had resisted but in the end, his father's decision held.

Teddy had been looking forward to a summer spent 'doing' his mind-fucked jock. Now Teddy was here and Brad was at home spending his summer training for his new career as a rookie cop. Teddy's recalled how hot his whipped stud looked in his baby cop blues and how he'd moaned in shame and desire as Teddy restrained him with his own academy issued cuffs while Teddy worked his hot officer's body over with his police regulation equipment. Hearing Brad begging was as much a turn on for him as it was for the young rookie now. A summer wasted Teddy grumbled to himself.

Oh well, Teddy thought, at least he had made sure Brad was going to be occupied. Teddy chuckled to himself as he recalled the look of horror and sensual lust that came to Brad's face when Teddy told him he had 'rented him out' to both a Latino and Black gang during his absence. Watching them bind the young rookie and test him out had been hot. Teddy could still visualize Brad all sexy and buff in his uniform getting cuffed; his tight bubble butt stretching out that, blue uniform pants; bent over a 'borrowed' police cruiser and getting fucked thru a slit they had put in its rear seam. Brad had shot a gusher through his blues leaving a large stain for all to see on the hood of the cruiser. Later one of the homeboys had pulled the hapless rookie over his lap for some old-fashioned bare-assed discipline. Brad's cries and whimpers as each guy took a turn warming his cute blonde cop-butt was a sight to behold. Brad had bawled like a baby pleading for them to stop but his rock hard throbbing dick told a different story. Brad's degradation had been total! Brad later confessed to Teddy that the thought of his white hole getting plowed repeatedly by their dark meat was humiliating and yet it drove him wild with desire. The blonde jock had so impressed the gang bangers with his performance they had gladly paid Teddy's asking price. Brad's look of utter humiliation coupled with frenzied craving as he was led away like a prized bitch was priceless. Teddy was so caught up in that recollection he never noticed that someone was speaking to him. Suddenly he felt a tap on his shoulder.

"Hey you skinny excuse for a kid I'm talking to you," a husky voice drawled to Teddy.

The teenager turned and found himself face to face with a powerfully built dark haired man. "Boy," the man said in a mocking tone, "you better keep it sharp mentally. I'm here to pick you up. I'm your uncle's foreman and I'm here to get you. Now get your gear and come with me!" The cowboy looked Teddy over. "Not much to you boy," he laughed heartily.

Teddy gave the man a once over as well. The cowboy standing before him had broad shoulders, powerful arms snug in a checked shirt, dark hairs coming out from under the shirt collar, tapered waist, thick brown curly hair and green eyes set in a ruggedly handsome yet sensual face. Early thirties at best as well as defiantly smug and confident. As the man turned to walk back to the truck, Teddy's gaze was riveted on his beefy butt and muscular thighs that strained the worn jeans. The muscles rippled seductively under the faded denim. This guy was hot Teddy thought as he climbed into the passenger seat.

"The name is Jake but you a call me boss like the other guys working here you got it. Your uncle is away on a buying trip for this summer and he told me to treat you like any wrangler here," Jake said roughly.

Teddy grimly contemplated what he heard. This was going to suck. The truck bounced along the road. Jake adjusted the clutch and Teddy couldn't help noticing the guy's tightly packed crotch as it shifted with each movement of those powerful legs. It was obvious that Jake had an impressive sack and judging, from the outline along his thigh under the faded denim, he had a good-sized rod as well. He wondered how hung the guy was and suddenly realized that Jake was aware of the direction of his gaze. He looked up quickly to see disgust registered on the handsome foreman's face. "Yeah I heard from your uncle about that too." Jake spat out, "going break you out of that shit boy. Turn you into a man."

Teddy sat silently fuming. He was a man.

"Boy," Jake lectured on in an arrogant superior tone, "I can't see how a guy can get off on dick." The handsome cowboy smirked. "Well, maybe if it was mine. Got me a real cunt cracker if I do say so myself." Jake reached down and crudely cupped his bulge. "Ain't never failed me yet in the female area. But dick sucking a dude. Fuck, let me tell you if some guy tried to get me to lick dick or even tried to dick my ass. Hell, I'd beat-up his sorry butt. I ain't no dick slobbering pussy-assed faggot."

Teddy steamed. He glanced at Jake. Hot, desirable and a total arrogant ass hole. He was just a more mature version of the old Brad and at that moment, Teddy knew what he intended to do about it. He remembered that he had packed some drugs and a small portable brain simulator and shipped it to a storage facility he had located here on cyber just on some off-chance. Looking at the sensual stud next to him Teddy realized that he had found his next pupil. "I'm looking forward to working with you boss and learning how a man like you acts." Teddy stated firmly.

Jake nodded at Teddy. "Good boy. Glad to hear it. It will all work out I think." The hunky foreman smiled suggestively. "You do well and I promise you that I'll make sure you get some tail okay."

"You got a deal boss," Teddy, laughed. "Going to be a kick-assed summer for us both!"

The two laughed as the truck bounced along to the ranch. Yeah boss, Teddy contemplated I'll get some tail but it wasn't going to be the tail you expect.

Part Two:
Cattle Drive Setup

Teddy was totally frustrated. It had been six weeks since he had arrived at his uncle's ranch. Six long work filled weeks working under Jake's ball busting as the humpty foreman continued his efforts to 'make a man' out his boss' nerdy nephew. Teddy was aching to conquer the handsome arrogant cowboy but so far, there had been no opportunity to get him alone for any amount of time. So Teddy just plotted, planned, and hoped for a chance.

Meanwhile Jake rode herd on his personal project. Today Teddy was digging posts with Jake. It was hot as hell and Jake had stripped to just his jeans. Teddy stared at the sculpted chest of his tormentor with its hard pecs and stunning eight pack that tapered down into a narrow waist. The curly dark chest hair was damp and glistened with Jake's sweat. Teddy could see the cowboy's jeans ride up into his crotch as he squatted to push a post into place. Jake noticed Teddy noticing and he shook his handsome chiseled features in disgust.

"Boy," he drawled. "I fucking hate faggots. I mean some guy slobbering over dick or worse taking up his shit-hole like some pussy. Never see this bull behaving like some heifer!" He chuckled as he adjusted his jeans. "Fucking some pussy that's the life for me. Especially if she is ah...well a bit reluctant." Jake hooted. "Never find this guy going down that dick slobbering pussy-assed faggot route!"

Teddy didn't reply. So far Jake had not come out and accused Teddy of being, as he referred to it at times, a "dick sucker" but Teddy knew only the fact his uncle was the boss kept Jake silent.

"I been trying these last few weeks to make a man out you," he grumbled to Teddy as they finished. "But I think you need a more intensive personal concentration from me."

Teddy looked at the hunky stud in puzzlement.

"There are some cattle up in the highlands that need to be herded in and branded," Jake grinned. "Going to take you up there. Just you and me boy for the next two weeks alone at the cabin up there. Going make a man out you yet. Got it!"

Teddy couldn't believe his ears. Eureka!

"Yep," Jake laughed. Going bust your ass up there but you'll come back a changed man."

Teddy smiled and nodded. Well Jake was right he thought but not in the way, he figured.

The next day the two of them set out for the cabin. Jake had ordered Teddy to prepare the gear for the trip and Teddy had complied. Jake had bragged to the rest of the cowboys on the ranch that he was going to break Teddy of his fagot habits and turn him into a real man! "That nerdy geek needs some lessons in how a man acts. Some broncs just need the right guy in the saddle to get broken in real sweet, and I'm just the guy to whoop his ass into shape!"

As they went on their trip, Teddy smiled in anticipation. On the last leg of the trail, the path up the trail narrowed at one point; as they rode up single file Teddy gazed at Jake's meaty butt and sighed with expectation. It was so fuckably firm and round.

"What you doing back there boy," Jake asked as he pulled out his canteen and gulped down the cold liquid inside.

"Just admiring the view," Teddy replied as he watched Jake gulp more of the contents. Teddy smiled. He had laced Jake's canteen with an extra strong drug combination. Soon Jake's sex drive and addiction centers would kick into overdrive causing his pliability levels to equally rise to the appropriate stage for mental realignment. "Well enjoy it now boy cause there is going to be some real ass busting once we get to the cabin," Jake grumbled in disgust.

"Yes I believe it," Teddy replied softly. He watched the muscles of Jake's throat gulp the wet concoction and visualized other things they would soon savor!

"And remember we are up here to get cattle and put our brand on their rumps boy," Jake pontificated. "You know you own 'em when they got your brand on their ass boy."

"I understand," Teddy agreed as ideas formed in his brain.

"And boy remember we only brand cows not bulls so watch yourself," Jake laughed.

They rode on as the trail opened onto the plain. Teddy rode alongside Jake now. Teddy noticed that as they did that Jake was fidgeting on his horse. Judging by the way his crotch was swelling as it rubbed against the leather saddle Jake was feeling the effects quite nicely.

"Everything ok sir," Teddy inquired.

Jake turned to Teddy with glassy eyes. "Yeaahh of coursth," he slurred. "Just hottt." The handsome foreman took another few gulps from his canteen. While they rode, Teddy could hear Jake's breathing quicken.

"Wow the air here is so fresh," smirked Teddy.

"Yeath," Jake mumbled as he gulped in more air and moved on his saddle trying to adjust his mound.

After ten more minutes in the saddle, Jake's crotch was obviously bulging and Teddy detected that Jake was squirming with frustration. In fact, the studly macho cowboy was literally rubbing against the saddle horn and panting in sexual arousal. "God," Jake groaned suddenly.

"You sure you are fine Jake?" Teddy cooed,

"Huh," Jake replied as his unfocused eyes tried to fix on Teddy. "I'm...fffffiiinnn...I mean..." his face was damp with perspiration. His muscular thighs were squeezing against his horse now. "Feeling... oh fuckkkkk." Jake mumbled incoherently as he began to literally hump his leather saddle. "Soooo... waaarrmm."

"Its ok Jake, just relax and take some more from that canteen," Teddy laughed as the cabin came into view." We got a lot of work to do these two weeks.

Jake tried to respond but just let out a weak whimper. He raised the canteen to his full lips and finished the contents. As he did, his crotch pressed even more lewdly against the saddle horn. The zapped foreman was gasping by now for sexual relief. As he massaged his rock hard cock against the firm saddle horn, he saw Teddy staring at him. He gazed down at his actions and blushed. "Got to cum so fucking bad." He blurted out. "I'm ...what's happening to me?" He moaned.

"It alright," Teddy said as they pulled up to the cabin. "Just relax and do as I say and it will be alright. I'll set you down on one of the bunk beds once we get inside."

"Allrith," Jake babbled as Teddy helped the drugged hunk out of his saddle and into the cabin. Jake's impressive rod was tent-poled in his jeans by now causing the faded material to strain across his meaty butt. Teddy grabbed Jake's butt and felt the hunky ass give to his grip. Jake just gasped, twitched, and then moaned in sexual heat. Teddy could see Jake was out of it by now and decided to 'test the waters'. He let go of Jake's ass and moved his hand to the front of the groaning foreman's jeans. Slipping one hand under the waistband in front and Teddy cupped Jake's hefty sack.

"Ooohhh mannn," Jake babbled as he literally trembled in

Teddy's grip on his nut-sack. "Don't stop please," Jake begged as he closed his eyes and gave into waves of sexual pleasure. The scrawny young geek had his muscular tormentor by the balls and the macho cowboy was squealing in delight! Jake reached down and rubbed his throbbing cock through the jeans. Teddy had seen it once when Jake had gotten out of the shower and knew that it was an impressive uncut 9 inches.

"Give in to it Jake", Teddy whispered to his handsome prey as Jake writhed under the twin actions of Teddy's ball play and his own palm job on his cock. "Ohhhh Teddddyyyy," Jake pleaded as he lost it. "I'm...FUCCCKKKKKK," Jake cried loudly as he lurched and spasmed. A wet spot appeared in his crotch. The air filled with the sucking sounds of Jake refilling his lungs. He was drenched in sweat and shaking in shame. A part of his smug brain registered that he had popped his nut under the touch of another man!

"Got you," Teddy chuckled as the formerly smug foreman turned beat red in embarrassment, "I'll just tie you up a bit on that bed and then go out back and start the outside generator so I can use the things I brought okay boy.

Jake couldn't focus on Teddy. He knew he should be resisting but he was all fuzzy in his brain and so turned on. He tried to swing at Teddy but his movements were so slow the young skinny kid was easily able to grab his hand and redirect it back onto his own crotch. It felt so good rubbing his own rod he couldn't stop. "Aaaahhh...yyeeahhh," Jake whimpered at he felt himself up.

"Good boy," Teddy howled in glee, "by the time I'm done with you Jake old boy you'll really get off on the touch of a man. Yes Mr. Macho Straight Foreman the days of you being head bull on the ranch are over but your days of being the local heifer are just beginning."

Teddy's laughter filled the cabin as he shut the door! During the next two weeks however it was the dull hum of electricity combined with sexual grunts and moans that not only filled the cabin but also the plain on which it was built

Epilogue

"Let's make sure you are set now," Teddy laughed as he tightened the ropes that bound a naked Jake to his saddle. Teddy stepped back to admire his work. Jake was nicely astride his saddle now. His legs were cinched around the back of his leather saddle and his arms were tied tightly to the neck of the horse. "Yes, that should do it" Teddy smiled. Jake's naked butt was up in the air with his crotch mashed tight onto the saddle's hot leather seat. Teddy figured that as the horse rode and moved the saddle would rub against Jake's dick giving the mind-fucked hunk a continuous masturbation. "By the time you get back to the bunkhouse you should be one cum drained cowboy," Teddy snickered.

"NNnnoooo plleeassee dooonn'tttt," Jake whimpered as he struggled and moved on the saddle. Thoughts of how the other wranglers would see their macho foreman like this and realize that the small younger boy had taken him down mentally and sexually sent shivers of embarrassment through him. The degradation he felt only intensified an arousal causing his meat to rise under him. Jake found himself pressing and then rubbing his dick on the saddle seat. The friction was unbearably sensual on his over sensitized rod. He couldn't resist moving to increase the sensations. Teddy noticed that Jake had begun to hump on the leather.

"Easy there girl," Teddy mocked as he patted Jake's ass like he saw the guys do with young female colts they wanted to steady as they got ready to break her in. Teddy knew the words and this particular type of physical contact would convey that same meaning to Jake. Hearing that word, especially in its feminine use, in combination with that action would further humiliate the hunky cowboy and thus increase his sexual submission.

"Ffffuuuccc...stoppppp," Jake groaned as his body betrayed him to its overwhelming new urges. The kid was further busting his bronc, treating him like a fucking filly and, Jake knew it.

"That's ok girl," Teddy cooed. "We know that you like something hard to suck on. That saddle horn looks tasty girl."

Without thinking, Jake suddenly found himself licking the saddle horn by his mouth. He heard Teddy's roar of laughter and he felt ashamed of how he needed to obey. Even as he criticized himself, his cock stiffened and he wiggled harder on the leather under him.

"Uummmpphhh," he muttered as he orally serviced that hard long horn in his mouth to satisfy his raging hard-on!

Teddy stroked his palm across Jake's rump. His finger slipped between Jake's spread thighs to give his exposed rosy pucker a nice massage as well. Jake tried not to make a noise but Teddy distinctly heard a soft mewing now from his filly. Teddy decided to give his filly a treat and inserted a finger deep in Jake's chute.

"Nooo…ooohhh…ffuccc," Jake sighed as his gyrations increased slightly in response to the finger fucking. "Noooo…nnnoooo… nooooooohhhhh," Jake babbled as he raised his ass to push back on Teddy's finger. Without realizing it Jake began to suck deeper onto the saddle horn as well." Ummmmmm uuummmmm uuummmm," Jake slobbered.

"Good girl," Teddy whispered. Yeah despite his protests, the handsome foreman was in heat once more. He liked being screwed now! Even more, he enjoyed sucking something while it happened! But there was one final touch.

"Oh yeah I almost forgot." Teddy chuckled as he went back to get out something from his saddlebag. Teddy returned with a small object and started to heat it with a lighter he had also brought.

"Hu," Jake croaked as he rubbed his engorged cock on the increasingly warm leather under him while he sucked on the horn. He had never been so horny and knowing that Teddy was seeing him act like a bitch in heat only made him hotter. He was lost in those desires and humiliations when he suddenly felt a burning pain on his exposed left butt cheek. He pulled off the saddle horn and bellowed. "AAAAAAAAAAAAAAAHHHHHHHHHHHHH FUCCCKKKK!" The valley echoed his screams and the hunky cowboy then passed out.

"Well after all you told me we had to brand every cow before we left right?" Teddy hooted as he inspected the small 'T' brand he had put on Jake's meaty butt. He revived Jake. "Now we go home!" Teddy said as he mounted his horse and grabbed the reins of Jake's horse, led his pony boy to home and the waiting ranch hands. "Let's take the rougher trail to give you a good workout on that saddle okay girl?" Jake lifted his head and nodded dully at his conqueror. He could feel the wetness under him. During the process, he had shot his wad! Jake, the tough swaggering ladies-man, had been ass whooped by the scrawny young boy but good! He was what a short time ago he had sworn he'd never be: a dick slobbering pussy-assed faggot. The ride home was filled with the sounds of the leather saddle getting a good soaking with Jake's climaxes. By the time, they pulled into the corral that saddle was saturated. The other wranglers were amazed, shocked, but then delighted that it had been their 'macho bragging ball-busting' foreman that had been taken on and trounced. From now on, he'd be every wrangler's bitch. That night the ranch's newest filly got saddled and mounted repeatedly by the wranglers he had lorded it over. The morning saw a butt fucked and dazed Jake lying naked and drenched on the floor of the bunkhouse. For the rest of the summer he serviced every cowboy on request. A good time was had by all!

DE-ALPHA DOGGED: TEDDY AND THE LT.

Part One:
New Turns

Teddy was bored. It had been three weeks since he had returned from the ranch and so far, he had not been able to hook up with Brad. It appeared Brad was on some law enforcement undercover assignment and was 'out of touch' for at least another month. No one had seen him, not even the gangs that had 'rented' him from Teddy for the summer. Three long weeks without any fun! Teddy sighed in his bedroom as he recalled his last day at the ranch especially that night with Jake. Teddy could still see that formerly smug hunky foreman tied spread eagle on the bunk bed. His hot muscular body draped over that old saddle with his beefy butt high up in the air begging to be plowed yet again. God thought Teddy that good old former straight boy really liked having his butt popped now particularly if while getting it he was spanked, tied, and, sprawled over his own saddle. The other ranch hands were practically wearing themselves out trying to satisfy Jake's newly implanted craving for dick. "Fuck me Teddy please," Jake had pleaded that night over and over. It got so annoying Teddy had called in another wrangler to fill Jake's mouth so he could screw the muscular foreman in some peace. Next to a good butt-fuck, Jake was crazy for sucking now.

Funny, Teddy thought, how the macho swaggering homophobic foreman had taken so well to man-sex in the end, especially when it was combined with anything that caused him to feel degradation or humiliation. That got him hotter than the proverbial pistol! The night they'd all forced Jake to cross-dress and parade around the bunkhouse had been a classic. Jake had been so turned on and so eager in his sexual services that the other wranglers had walked bow-legged the entire next day. Thinking back on all that fun only made Teddy more eager to contact Brad. He called the academy where Brad was posted but got the same reply to every call Teddy had made numerous times before.

The young rookie was on a special assignment and not able to be contacted. Teddy recalled how he had punked the handsome blonde police recruit when they had been in school together. The scrawny Teddy had enjoyed conquering the haughty muscular straight jock and reducing him to a cock crazed submissive. Remembering Brad's tight ass and hunky body made Teddy horny as hell. He needed sex. It would soon come.

Later that day the doorbell rang. When Teddy answered it, he found himself face to face with a uniformed State Trooper.

"Are you Teddy," the officer asked gruffly. Teddy nodded. "I'm Lt. Bill Evans from the State Police investigative unit. Our station was contacted by the police academy commander. You've been trying to reach an officer for some reason. I'm here to ascertain that reason."

Teddy gazed the man standing there before him. Lt. Evans appeared to be in his early thirties. At 6'4" he towered over Teddy. That he was extremely well built was obvious from the way his body stretched his tight brown uniform. The uniform's color only accentuated the light mocha complexion of the officer. Teddy had never seen such a handsome man before. As he gazed into the mirrored sunglasses the Lt wore, Teddy could see his own hungry reflection. It was obvious Teddy realized that he was turned on. If Teddy could see that so, no doubt, did the officer. A sneer came to the trooper face.

"Looks like I got a reason already," he replied to his own question. "WE better talk!"

"My dad's not home," Teddy mumbled. "He's at a weeklong conference."

"I think that will make our talk franker." He said condescendingly as he removed his glasses to reveal eyes golden in color. The officer pushed past Teddy to walk in. As Teddy followed, the trooper into the living room Teddy got an excellent look at the Lt.'s perfectly shaped butt. Lt. Bill Evans was a true stunner and a prize Teddy decided he would have!

"Okay Teddy," the handsome officer said in a deeply sexy growl as he sat down in a chair. "I'm going to tell you what is what and not pull any punches. In fact, if you repeat what I'm going to tell you I'll deny it. Got it!"

Teddy couldn't help gazing at the well-rounded package the officer had. The tight uniform pants he was wearing had risen up as the officer sat down to cup nicely around the hefty location. The Lt. had to be packing some major equipment down there Teddy realized.

"Hey faggot, my eyes are up here," the trooper said loudly.

Teddy was startled and surprised at the slur being used so freely. He stared up at the Lt. who by now was shaking his head in disgust. Yeah he was going to do him.

"Good boy," the trooper said condescendingly. "Listen I could give a rat's ass if you and this rookie you've been trying to contact are a pair of fudge packers okay." The officer stated forcefully. "Quite frankly I having seen the officer in question I can't think of what he'd see in you even if he is a cock-licker," Evans smirked. Teddy fumed but stayed silent. "I mean no offense but you are a nerd if ever I saw one while the rookie in question is a true jock type. Pity he's a fag though. Oh well" the officer laughed. "The rookie is on a major assignment so stop bothering everyone or I'll bust your ass, got it boy!"

Teddy signaled his understanding as his mind raced to figure out a plan. But sometimes the heavens open for us. Today they did again.

"Good." Evans smiled causing him to look even more handsome if that was possible Teddy thought. "Glad you got the message. Now I will be on my way." The Lt. put on his glasses. "Oh, mind if I get some water. Been along drive and it's hot out there?"

Teddy beamed. "No sir, my pleasure sir." Teddy smiled as he raced into the kitchen.

"Good kid. Glad we had this talk. No offense now." Evans said from the living room as Teddy poured a cold glass of water laced with a triple dose of his handy tasteless drug.

Teddy returned and glass the glass to the Lt. who gulped the contents down briskly.

"Thank you sir for coming to see me and setting me straight." Teddy replied in mock sincerity as he anxiously awaited the drug to kick in.

"Setting you straight," giggled Lt. Evan as the drug swiftly grabbed hold. "Faggots," the hunky young officer muttered as he slowly staggered toward the door only to slump back into Teddy's waiting embrace.

Teddy lowered his newest prey to the floor. Lt. Bill Evans lay there in all his handsome muscular glory. A true sensual sight in his tight trooper uniform and mirrored glasses. A peaceful smile was on his lips. "Oh yes," Teddy said to himself as he dragged the unconscious drugged trooper to his 'special' playroom. "I guess you didn't set me straight after all Lt."

Part Two:
Smile for the Pretty Birdie

For the next two hours, Teddy was a buzz of activity. First, he had dragged the doped trooper to his 'special room' and made sure the unconscious stud was firmly tied to the table he kept there. Then Teddy had used his computer skills to secretly hack into the state police data bank. Once in he surfed to the call in message center to 'post' a received call-in from Lt. Bill Evans explaining that a sudden illness had struck him on duty and that he was taking a few days of off-duty time. Lastly, a quick hop to personnel records had enabled Teddy to download the humpy officer's personnel file with its helpful physiological profile.

According to the detailed reports, Lt. Bill Evans was a single 32-year-old wonder boy. Raised by doting parents in a middle-class neighborhood, he had excelled in school and sports. In fact, the young officer had bragged to the interviewer during his academy screening session that he had never tasted defeat in any competition of a one-on-one nature. The pyschological profile had noted that the rookie had a classic view of manhood in which a man was dominate in life and in bed. There was a subtle but unmistakable view that a real man bedded women and that men who got bedded and, in his opinion, 'gave up their butts willingly to other guys' were somehow pathetic and weak. The future trooper had taken great pains to comment on his sexual prowess as if his multiple female 'scoring' somehow reaffirmed his masculinity. It also seemed that the Lt. had a low view of what he called 'ghetto home-boys trash'. The officer's comments to questions seemed rather smug to Teddy. Teddy wondered how the arrogant officer would react to being bested in a competition.

On the whole however the young hunk had impressed his superiors by his firm belief that being a trooper was a big responsibility and that any cop who disgraced his uniform was, in his words, 'lower than low'. It was clear that the female interviewer had glossed over the possible chinks in the mental armor of the young hunk. Teddy wondered if perhaps the interviewer had succumbed to the rather obvious physical charms of the subject. In any event, Teddy had the weapons he needed now. He turned and gazed at the zonked captive. Running his hand down the sleeping officer's chest toward his basket Teddy plotted his moves.

"Going to truly enjoy this," Teddy chuckled as his hand cupped the Lt.'s family jewels. He unzipped the officer's pants and pulled out the contents underneath. Lt. Evans was packing some major equipment alright. His nuts were hefty and full; his rod was an uncut thick monster even in its flaccid state. Teddy did a quick hand-job to get the officer's 'full measure'. It was, once aroused, quite impressive. The drugged hunk gave out a deep guttural moan of approval." Yeaaaaahhh... ohhh yeaahh," he grunted as his hips rose up to literally fuck his meat in Teddy's grip. A look of contentment came to his handsome sun-glassed face as his rod stiffened to its full height. "Ohh yeahhh," the Lt gasped as he bucked faster. Seeing the trooper in full uniform with an exposed hard-on gave Teddy an idea. He quickly ran to get a camera. A few minutes later Teddy had pictures of the sexy looped trooper in full uniform with one hand now freely pumping his own exposed erect manhood, and judging from the smile on his face, having the time of his life while pleasuring himself.

Teddy smirked as he inserted a dildo in the trooper's mouth, arranged the Lt.'s other free hand to grip it and, set it up to look as if the still aroused law officer was enjoying some oral fun. Teddy managed to even get an impressive money-shot as the Lt., with a strangled cry, blew his wad for the camera. Lastly Teddy flipped the Evans over, lowered his uniform to his knees, and propping up his hard bubble butt made it seem that the still smiling Lt. was using the dildo to do a number on his ass. "I wonder how you will react to seeing how you just disgraced your uniform boy." Teddy laughed. After a few more shots, Teddy was ready to begin his newest conquests.

"Party time Lt. Evans," he said as he stripped the studly officer in preparation for wiring, drugging, and ultimate defeat.

Part Three:
He Yields

Bill Evans had awakened to find himself tied to a table in some room. Everything was still fuzzy. He remembered meeting with some fag kid to check on his connection with a new recruit in the police department; discovering the recruit was a fag too; his getting up to leave but then it all got hazy. Now he found himself tied spread eagled and naked. He pulled at the ropes. It must have been that fag he thought but how the hell had that skinny fruit overpowered him. As he struggled, he realized that parts of his body had patches on them from which wires ran to a machine in the corner. The patches were on each of his nipples and, judging from the prickling sensations, he felt, behind his nuts and at the base of his brain. He felt a tingling current flowing through them to his body. It was not an unpleasant experience in fact, he found it stimulating even arousing. That sudden thought instantly left him in shock. Arousing, no way! But, as he looked down his body toward his crotch, he realized that his nipples were firm and worse he was sporting an impressive hard-on as well. "What the fuck is going on," he roared!

"Just a little training exercise Lt." a voice from behind him said quietly. The state trooper tried to turn his head but couldn't see the person who had spoken. In a second, however the speaker moved into his line of sight. It was that fruity faggot kid!

"You sick pansy you are so fucked," the hunky cop roared as he pulled at his bindings. His efforts to break free only emphasized his hard muscularity.

"Oh someone is going to be that," Teddy laughed as he quickly inserted a needle into one of the law officer's bulging biceps to inject him with a liquid. Teddy moved to the machine and increased the output. A hot sensual electrical vibration flushed through the restrained captive. Lt. Evans found that his nipples responding even more now as they rose and hardened into reddish-brown mounds while his nuts vibrated with each volt that hit them.

"What the fuck is going on?" the bound stud moaned. Lt. Evans pulled and jerked at his restraints not comprehending that the physical exertions merely speeded the drugs through his system. Teddy gazed at his captive. The additional drug dosage would over stimulate the primary sexual drives of its victim while the electrical currents being delivered to his nipples and nuts would arouse those erogenous zones in tandem. More importantly, the ones attached to his head would energize the addictive centers in the lawman's brain.

"Oh fuck," the bound cop, sighed. He had never been as turned on before. The drugs combined with the electrical stimulations were sending him into an even more aroused condition. He didn't realize that beyond the outward signs of his sexual arousal his brain was taking notes and feeding his control circuits even as his addictive centers were processing this need.

"Let's, as some cook says, kick it up a notch," Teddy smirked as he increased the current and gave a booster shot to the hunky black cop.

The captured trooper soon felt an even stronger warm wave engulf his body. The electrical impulses became even more arousing and soon his cock was achingly stiff. The thought that this pathetic kid was seeing him in such a depraved sexual state filled him with shame. He was completely turned on however and they both knew it. That thought only increased his emotional degradation. In some deeper recesses of his brain, the twin sensations of shame and sexual arousal registered. A tenuous connection between the two began to imprint on his psyche.

Teddy looked at the erection on his trooper. It was clear that the man needed to erupt. Teddy lightly ran his fingers along the sensitive underside of Evan's thick dark monster. The flesh was moist and wet from the copious pre-cum that was leaking out of it. He gently rubbed up and down the shaft with his fingertips finally letting his thumb massage the dark head of the trooper's rod.

"Ooooohhhh fuucckkkk." The captured hunk squirmed as his balls churned inside his hefty dark nut sack to this new physical contact. Teddy noticed that unlike the light skin tone of the trooper's body his 'jewels' were darker in color. "Stop that," Bill gasped as his rod quivered for release. His round head darkened considerable in reply to Teddy's touch.

"Oooooooo mmmaaannnnnn," he grunted as the urge to erupt hit him full force. He was hotter than ever before. No woman's touch had gotten him this inflamed. His current state of excitement had short-circuited any logic that would have enabled him to see it was the drugs that were the cause of his heightened senses. In his drug-disabled mind, it was Teddy, a guy, who was getting him hard and that thought was driving him crazy and chipping away at his macho self-image. He hated thinking he was sexually excited by another guy but it was clear he was. His body, in response to this arousal, was pumping out endorphins and his now fully active addiction centers inside him printed the pattern for future use. The young hapless black Lt. was gradually being addicted these new experiences. "Got... tooooo... ooohhh ssttttooopppppppp." He whimpered even as his hips instinctively thrust up so that his raging cock could press firmly against Teddy's palm.

"Really?" Teddy teased as he stroked the law officer's roaring hard-on. Teddy was gratified by the moan that escaped from his 'trainee'.

"Fffffuuuuuuccccckkkkkkk," the cop babbled incoherently.

Teddy smiled and looked into the officer's bleary eyes. The handsome young black trooper could barely focus on Teddy. "I'm willing to help you get some...ah relief but if you prefer not too?"

"Take... your... faggaahh... hhaannddss... ooffaawwww," the officer panted as the twin effects of the drugs and electrical currents that were raising his sexual temperature to the breaking point. He hated that this kid was touching him, arousing him, and thus humiliating him in the process. He despised it all yet a part of him wanted to get-off so badly now and that part knew the skinny kid now manipulating his engorged pole was the only one who could do it for him at this juncture. His control/addiction centers noticed the conflicting emotions of increasing desire and overwhelming shame and their connection firmed inside his brain.

"You sure," Teddy said as he changed his grip and began to pump the trooper's rod. The effect was instantaneous as the bound officer's eyes went glossy. He was losing control fast. "Tell me you want it."

"Oh god yesss," the officer finally hissed as he felt himself approaching climax. He wanted to cum and thoughts of a guy getting him off were now irrelevant. But just as he was, about to erupt the young boy applied pressure to the base of the officer's dick in a way that cut off his climax and left him painfully unfulfilled. The macho trooper's brain and body screamed with frustration." FUCK NOOOOOOOOOOOHHH!" He howled.

"Ask me nicely." Teddy replied, "And I might just help you relieve that need."

The young law officer's cock remained rigid. "Please," he whined in despair. "Please get me off." He had to cum. He couldn't endure not blowing his wad by now. Teddy smiled. The strapping and arrogant black stud was breaking. It was time to hand him his first defeat!

"Will you do as I ask?" Teddy smirked as he quietly disrobed.

By now, the once smug Lt. was lost in arousal. He barely registered that Teddy was now naked; he wanted relief and he wanted Teddy to give it to him. His mind however registered every emotion and distress. "I need to cum. I need to cum so bad please," he begged.

"You called me a cock-licker," Teddy stated with disgust. "You want to cum then lick my cock!" Teddy climbed on top of the prone trooper straddling him in a way that enabled him to keep his own cock right by the officer's mouth but still retaining the ability to reach back to pump the Lt.'s erection.

The good-looking captive felt the sensual warmth of Teddy's ass on his chest. The light body hairs of the skinny kid's legs pleasurably ticked his now over sensitized nipples. It felt so fantastic he maneuvered his chest's pectorals so they could rub Teddy's thighs. "Oh yeahhhhh," he groaned as his nipples got gratification.

"Enjoying this huh," Teddy smiled as he flexed his thighs across the trooper's nipples. He gazed into the black cop's eyes. They were glossy. No doubt, now, he thought, this stud is primed. He reached back running his palm down the cop's eight pack and following the sparsely haired dark curly honey trail to his objective. He enclosed the cop's dark meat in his hand and began to pump.

"Lick my cock boy," Teddy whispered as he rested his erection on the young Lt.'s lips.

"Please... not... suckk dicckkkk," Bill whined once more. He heard his tone and cringed at how pathetic he sounded. Yet his body became more aroused by that concept.

"Lick it." Teddy repeated as he lifted some pre-cum from his own cock and smeared it along the red full lips of the restrained former jock. The salty taste oozed into the Lt.'s mouth. The taste embarrassed him but to his brain, that was now the signal for a corresponding surge of pleasure. More endorphins kicked in and the battle was won.

The muscular cop's body heaved a sigh. "Fuck." Lt. Bill Evans the once haughty homo hating state trooper stared up in defeat at his conqueror. Silently he opened his mouth and accepted Teddy's cock. As his throat learned the proper art of sucking, a dick Teddy slowly stroked the cop's own demanding meat.

"Hmmmmm," the officer gurgled as he savored an overpowering rush of sexual satisfaction while he blew Teddy. Never rushing Teddy made sure that the stud learned how to suck, registered precisely what he was doing, and most importantly experienced sexual gratification while he was doing it.

"More...more...more," The formerly straight officer pleaded at one point as he pulled off Teddy's cock. Teddy quietly guided the handsome hunk's face back onto his rod and quickened his own hand job on the officer. The Lt. slurped and suctioned Teddy's dick with a newfound eagerness. He was so turned on. The debasement of sucking a guy's dick was more than compensated in the face of the erotic thrill that was coursing though him. His mind registered that this was the hottest sex it had ever experienced and his addiction centers intertwined that fact, the degradations being experienced and, the endorphin high it was getting from all this into a abiding craving. The homophobic cop was to be permanently addicted to this type of man on man sex now although that realization was to come later for him!

Finally the long sought for climax occurred. With a muffled roar, the young Lt. erupted. "AAAAAARRRGGGGHHHHHH!"

Teddy came as just at that moment as well thus enabling the hunky Lt's fried brain to forever assume that its own pleasurable ejaculation was intimately tied in with giving head and swallowing another guy's jism.

For the next few hours, Teddy repeated this fundamental lesson for his captive. By nightfall, a weary Lt. Bill Evans left Teddy's house with a total addiction to sucking dick especially if in the process of doing so he was being humiliated and abused.

Teddy watched the trooper drive off. He turned and strolled back into the room. He had some pictures to print and plans to make.

For Lt. Evans the days passed. He couldn't forget what had happened to him at Teddy's. Every time he recalled what he had done, he found he got an impressive hard-on. He arrived at the state barracks to find a package for him. He sat at a back desk and opened it. Inside were pictures of him in full uniform posed in sexually humiliating poses. Included was a tape that contained the sex sounds of his night with Teddy. There were instructions to meet Teddy that night in a deserted warehouse. He was to be dressed in his best uniform as well. It seemed that Teddy had something more to teach his handsome black stud. Bill Evan's broke out into a cold sweat but he also realized that he was as hard as a rock. He looked around to make sure he wasn't in any observable position then unzipped and beat himself off while he gazed at the pictures and remembered the taste of Teddy's manhood as it ravished his throat. He came with a stifled cry. "Yessss," he hissed to himself.

As he cleaned up, he thought 'I'm a cock-sucker'. His handsome faced flushed with a shame that only seemed to arouse him more. What more could happen to him he muttered to himself. Little did he know!

That night the officer entered the warehouse. To his surprise he encountered not just Teddy but the academy rookie Brad along with a group of gang bangers as well.

"Hi Billy-boy," Teddy laughed, "ready to continue your cock sucking?" The Lt. cringed with humiliation at hearing this taunt especially in front of the gang members. Unfortunately, his body responded in a completely different way as a rather noticeable erection began to sprout in his uniform pants. He was now totally embarrassed and with that emotion an overwhelming arousal engulfed him. A faint wet spot appeared in his crotch, which only inflamed his sexual cravings for more!

"See guys he likes it just like Brad here," Teddy informed the amazed gang members. They couldn't believe it but the proof was there in the trooper's pants. A grin broke out on their faces as they recalled how the lighter-skinned law officer had lorded it over them on his patrols. Smug and demeaning to his darker-skinned bros and full of his own macho worth as a Lt. State Trooper he has always engaged in subtly putting them down at every step both for their lack of social status and darker complexions. Yet now here he was quietly accepting the taunts of some skinny cracker and obviously hot for it.

"Please," Bill pleaded to Teddy. "Not them." He felt lower than shit but that very emotion now spurred his arousal to a fever pitch.

"Pay back time," their leader nodded to Teddy. "Get over here bitch and kneel," he taunted as he pulled out his thick and uncut dick." Service this now!"

The formerly haughty trooper stared at the gang leader's impressively hung cock. Its dark shinny flesh sent shivers throughout his system. He remembered his old attitude toward darker black men and the thought that he'd be on his knees sucking a black cock filled him with horror. "No...I...won't...nooo," he protested but to his amazement, he found himself crawling over to the young homeboy and meekly taking the gang leaders cock into his throat. The warehouse overflowed with the mocking howls of the gang boys as they lined up to get serviced by their newest cop slut.

"Hmmm...hmmmm...hmmm," the officer muttered as he tongue bathed the gang banger's dick. At one point, the trooper reached down to rub his own hard-on.

"No way you getting off bitch," the leader said as he enjoyed his triumph. He signaled a fellow gang member who approached and took the trooper's own cuffs and hand cuffed the young officer's hands behind his back. That extra humiliation of being restrained by his own cuffs only increased the Lt.'s craving for dick sucking. Something in him snapped and gave up. From that, second onward he would eagerly slobber over every cock presented to him. At one point, he got so aroused he creamed in his blues. He was completely degraded yet fantastically aroused.

As for Brad, just seeing the handsome superior officer being thoroughly pussied by gang bangers, and loving it as well, triggered his own programmed sex drive. He stood there quivering in his own world of sexual arousal. Teddy gave the slurping trooper one last injection of the drug he had brought and then, as the boys in the hood did their thing with the handsome officer, Teddy led his blonde cop recruit to a back room for some private service.

As Teddy let Brad service his joint, he listened as the gang boys did their thing on their former tormentor.

"Please Kahil not in my ass," Teddy heard the Lt. plead. "No one has ever fucked my...arrrrggghhhhhhh." Teddy smiled as he contemplated Kahil, the gang's humpy leader, doing the formerly arrogant trooper's cherry. Teddy face-fucked Brad with a new vigor as he visualized Kahil's hefty dark monster opening up Lt. Evans hole.

"Ugh. Ugh. Ugh," came the grunting sounds from Lt. Evans, as his butt was ravished. Once more, the lawman's body experienced the familiar sexual stimulations of the drug combined with the concurrent feelings of total humiliation. His brain just accepted it as an addition to the other prior programming and soon the hunky officer was as addicted to getting fucked as he was to sucking guys off. Almost immediately, he was moaning in heat so loudly the other gang bangers had to continuously plug his mouth with their cocks just to stop the noise.

"Umph. Umph. Umph," came the muffled cries of the cock crazy trooper as both ends of his muscular body were filled with the thick dark meat of his tormentors.

Teddy broke into a hug grin. He had won again!

The next morning the warehouse was left with the distinct smell of rutting due to both lawmen having been repeatedly plowed in every orifice they had.

Epilogue

Teddy shifted in his chair enjoying the spectacle of the uniformed formerly homophobic State Trooper kneeling before him now and meekly giving him head. The sight of the handsome studly Lt. lapping away on his balls and cock was hot as hell.

"You know Billy-boy," Teddy said enjoying the cringe effect using 'boy' had on the young hunky officer. "I think a double-fuck with Brad would be nice this weekend. I want you to pull some strings and get him here, you got it Billy-boy."

"Yes sir," replied Lt. Evans meekly as he carried on his slurping at Teddy's nuts. Bill Evans shuddered at the thought of how this scrawny young geeky teenager now controlled his butt. Part of him was appalled and humiliated at his total submissive behavior now but as the degradation of all this flooded his brain he found that it only made sexually servicing Teddy all the more desirable. The handsome officer gulped down Teddy's rod with renewed frenzy.

"Yeah maybe I'll let you eat out Brad's ass," Teddy mused out loud. "Like that thought? You a hot-shot Lt. eating a rookies butt?"

The hunky officer cringed but continued his oral work on Teddy. From the tent-pole in his uniform pants, it was clear Evans was turned on big time now! Teddy watched as 'Billy-boy' reached back under his police issued belt, down his pants, and between his bubble cheeks to push in further the butt plug Teddy insisted Bill wear whenever he was in uniform. "That's right Billy-boy. Just like, I taught you. Never let either hole be empty during sex. Maybe I'll invite some of my gang friends over. Yeah would you like that Billy-boy? Some of the homeboys from the old neighborhood. The guys you busted and looked down on now looking down on you as you service their dicks and rim their dirty holes once again?"

The trooper thought he should protest but the way he was greedily sucking now combined with how hard his own dick was pressing in his tight uniform showed him that the thought of that prospect was arousing as hell for him. A flush of shame filled him sending him into a dizzying fever of sexual craving. The arrogant Lt. was whipped and he knew it! He gurgled as he deep-throated his master in submission. His free hand unzipping his uniform pants to pull out and stroke his hard cop-meat as he contemplated servicing those homeboys he had always considered his inferiors.

"Show me how you State Troopers service the public." Teddy's laughter filled the house alongside the whimpering grunts of the handsome State Trooper as he pleasured his conqueror and satisfied his own degrading desires!

Postscript

Like all good plans, Teddy's had one fatal flaw. Kahil, the gang leader, had developed a thing for Teddy. He soon convinced Teddy to explain to him every step in the pussying of Lt. Evans. Unknown to Teddy the good-looking and built gang banger had an ulterior motive. As much as Kahil had enjoyed busting the trooper a part of him didn't really like that a brother, even an asshole like the officer, was now some white geek's sex slave especially a white geek that he secretly was hot for. One day, with his father on another trip, a knock came to the door. Kahil and a few of his boys took hold of Teddy and dragged him to that special room for treatment. Teddy is now blissfully serving as Kahil's personal white bitch. As for Brad and Bill, well every gang needs their bitches too! Don't feel too bad for Teddy for, if truth be told, Teddy inwardly had been lusting for Kahil since he first saw the homeboy's impressive dark rod. Though he had not wanted to admit it, our young friend was a closet bottom who had hoped Kahil would assert control over him and sexually bottom him. After awhile Kahil was as addicted to Teddy as Teddy was to him. In fact, he let Teddy continue to conquer and top other smug guys provided the geeky boy always came home to share his bed. So it all ended quite well and the two had some amazing sexual adventures!

DOGGING THE STATE TROOPER

Part One

I first saw him again when he came into my bar! I had just brought the local pub in the town. Not a big place but hell, but it suited my plans quite nicely. I was a man with a mission target and, his name was Mike the local state trooper assigned to this rural town by the central state police bureaucracy (with a little prodding from me and my friend "Ben Franklin" to the clerk at the assignment board).

He swaggered in like he owned the place. At 6'1" of solid built muscle, tampering into a 32-inch V waist poured into a pair of uniform blues that displayed his bubble butt he was impressive! When he came up to the bar all I could see was that dark black hair and green eyes. Yep he was a stunning looking hot stud alright, just as I remembered him from high school! I was a geeky computer wiz who idolized the school quarterback. He knew and used that to tease me unmercifully throughout our senior year. I promised myself I'd "score my own touchdown" on his hunky butt one day. After graduation, my family moved but I never forgot him. It was Mike and his payback that gave me the desire to make good. Well, I scored big in silcon valley with my own company. I used my money to find him, once I did I hired a trainer to get me buffed and with his help the geek became a new man. There was no way I would be recognized and it was then, I decided to accomplish the one thing I longed for...revenge!

For the next few weeks, I "played "the friendly bar keeps quick with a drink and easy conversation. Mike became a regular coming in just after his late shift for a beer. One night it was just him and me near closing time. I decided then to make my move! When he wasn't looking, I slipped a "special something" in his bottle and watched as he gulped it down. I just kept on talking with him watching as the drug took effect. His eyes started to glaze and beads of sweat appeared on his forehead.

"Gees," he mumbled slightly slurring, "Is it hot in here?"

I said nothing as he loosened his top collar button undid his tie and opened his shirt a bit exposing his curly dark chest hairs. If I had any doubts seeing that man chest fur curling around his neck convinced me to go for broke!

"Hey Mike," I replied sounding pure concern. "You look a bit tired my friend. Why don't you grab a few zzz's in my back room? No sense falling asleep at the wheel. Besides how would that look you being a trooper and all?"

He tried to focus on me but the drug was running full tilt by now, so all he could do was dully nod as if trying to think the offer over. I decided to press home!

I eagerly came up beside him and guided him into the room, "here you go officer," my voice oozing concern, "you just relax and rest here in the backroom till you feel better!"

He gazed at me through dilated pupils–yep, the drug was working, "thanks man," he slurred, "dam I feel dizzy?" I just smiled as I helped him onto the bed. In a few minutes, he was lying there out cold. As I looked down at his chest rising up and down in a slow breathing rhythm, I knew that tonight he was all mine!

Quickly I stripped good old Mike of his trooper gear till he was butt naked. I stared at his body for a while. I'll say this for him, he was one sculpted stud meat with hard chiseled chest and leg muscles, a six pack that felt rock hard, not to mention being hung with an uncut 9" monster of a cock combined with a set of balls that swayed in his low hanging bull sack. When I turned him over his butt was like a melon all ripe for the picking. I gently squeezed his cheeks and he sighed–yeah, I thought, you'll do more than sigh cop by the time I get done with you! I knew the drug would wear off fast so I got to work tying him down on the four-poster. I'd just finished when my trooper stirred.

"Oh my head", he moaned as he came to. "WHAT THE FUCK!" he yelled as he realized that he was hogtied! He struggled and bucked giving me a nice rear view of that cop butt cinching and flexing.

"Ok cop thats enough," I yelled behind him as I slapped that smooth bubble behind of his.

SLAP!

SLAP!

"HEY," he cried, now turning his head to face me, "let me go now buddy or your ass is mine!" he growled.

"I believe it's your ass that's mine here" I smirked. "Time to learn that mouth of yours better behave itself!"

SLAP!

SLAP!

With that, I began slapping that white ass of his. He bucked but I was relentless.

WACK!

WACK!

WACK! "NOOOOOOOO! ARGHHHHHH," he howled. "STOP IT!" with each slap he clenched his butt making my swat even better. The air filled with the sounds of my hits and his shrieks till at last... "Please stop," he moaned, "please man I'll behave please." As he begged, his eyes filled with tears. I had won the first round! My trooper was bawling like a baby – the breaking of this stud was underway!

"From now on its sir, you understand?"

"YES...sir" he mumbled!

"Couldn't hear you boy," I growled as I let another whack hit his red ass.

WACK!

"YES SIR!" he responded quickly.

"Good baby," I cooed as I rubbed his butt turning on to the heat coming off that now red cop bum. "As a reward for your obedience I have a surprise," with that, I reached into my pocket and pulled out a bottle containing something that the boys at my company had developed for me. A new little product that relaxed a person's inhibitions, put then into a sort of super high suggestibility stage, all while revving their sex drive into overtime!

"HUH," he said now totally confused and scared, "what surprise sir?"

I pushed the bottle under his nose before he realized what it was.

"What's that smell," he said the fumes filling his lungs" Noooo not... oh shit...my heads spinning...what was thattttttt," he slurred.

I watched as his eyes dilated under the drugs effects – laughing as a goofy grin broke out on his cop's face. Yea my trooper stud was flying without a net but I was eager to continue.

"How you feel stud boy," I asked letting him breathe in some more of the bottle while I held it close.

"OH shit sirrr," he garbled, "I feel soooo weird sir..." He relaxed onto the table blissfully sniffing the aroma in and sighing in peace. Oh, he was going nowhere now! Time for the next phase of my plans. I untied my drugged out stud.

"Upsie daisy there Mikie", I laughed as I flipped him over and helped him sit up. Mike was really out of it just sitting there with his hands in his lap looking at me with his zonked out green eyes!

"I feel so funny man," he slurred as he tried to stare at me. He looked down at his crotch and started to rub his dick, "damn," he whispered, "My dick feels funny too." He began to rub his monster dick while I watched it harden.

"That's right Mikee," I agreed putting the bottle under his nose," you just breathe deep and play with yourself ok while I set up this video. Here you hold the bottle to!" I had a video cam all ready. I set the camera on roll and watched as my trooper sniffed deeply from the bottle for the lens, gazing as his chest expanded with the fumes he was inhaling. Soon he was blissfully masturbating for the video. I was getting it all on tape while Mike jerked away moaning loudly as his cock stiffened to full length! I made sure the camera caught every moment of it especially the drug sniffing and druggie glazed eyeballs. Good old trooper Mike was going to be in big trouble if this got to his superiors but there was more to come!

"Hey Mike," I said muffling my voice, "got another surprise for you"

Mike looked at me smiling away in flight "another sir?" he asked all childlike.

"Yes, now open your mouth and close your eyes" I stated as I climbed on the table, careful to avoid getting my face on camera. Mike, now totally out of it complied quickly jaw dropping and eyelids closed! I unzipped my jeans freeing my cock and placed it right near his mouth, "I bet you're real thirsty huh?" He nodded, mouth open and tongue out... "Well try sucking this okay!" Slowly I inserted my head onto his tongue. Eyes closed he started to lick the head. I felt his wet moist heat on my dick and slowly eased into his waiting hole. He opened his eyes as I slipped in staring widely at me smiling. I smiled back as I began my mouth fuck making sure that the bottle was still by his nose! OH yeah! Mike took too it like a duck to water. His tongue rolled over and under my dick like a pro. The room filled with the sounds of my meat slapping into his mouth. As I gazed down, I saw that he was as hard as a rock and his hand was jerking himself off! The video camera was going full out as I face humped my cop while listening to his slurping sounds. Baby I was busting my straight boy right! I felt the incredible warmth of his throat on my dick. As I looked down, I could see his cop meat glistening with his pre jis. I saw that he was also working his trooper meat as well, pumping that shaft of his like it was an oil derrick. Suddenly, his mouth tightened and he went rigid, I knew then he was getting ready to explode so I grabbed my stallion by his head and drove my shaft in tight. He gurgled and reached up with one free hand pawing my hips but I was in tight. I heard a strangled moan from him, and he came like a geyser shooting his cream up over his six-pack. That did it for me; I came in gallons, flooding his canal as he slurped my jis up for dear life. When it was over, I eased him off my dick letting him plop back on the bed gulping in air. In a few seconds, he had drifted off to sleep totally exhausted and sleeping like a baby with his tongue licking the remnants of my cream off his lips. Seeing him like that, gave me an idea. I slicked his thumb over his stomach getting it wet with his stud juices and brought it up to his mouth. Sure enough, he went for it sucking his thumb like a newborn all smiling and peaceful. My camera got it all on tape. Watching my trooper infant cooing away as he sucked his thumb I planned out my next phase for him. Yes sir, good old trooper Mikie was on the roll of his life now...

A Boner Book

Part Two

It was quite a few hours later when Mike woke up. I had managed to get him dressed, carried my " baby" back to his car, and from there to his home. I knew that he would be back, if only to beat me to a pulp but I was prepared! Sure enough, later that day I heard him pull up to the bar (closed by me so we could have "privacy") and slam open the door.

"Where are you bastard," he yelled. "Your dead you hear me!"

I stepped out of the side room. He turned to face me and started forward, his hands clenching into fists. "I think before you do anything you should see this," I retorted as I pressed the video remote in my hand. The overhead bar screen flickered to life with good old Mike starring in the home movie. He gazed at the scenes of his performance in shock.

"Now listen, this goes to your station buddies unless you do as I say. Got it!" I replied.

Mike stared at me–hate burning in his eyes –then at the flickering images. He started breathing heavily as the barroom filled with his video moans. He looked back at the screen just as the thumb sucking section rolled on view. He uttered a strangled cry as the bar filled with the sucking sounds he had made along with his baby gurgling, all at once, a large sigh left him, his fists unclenched, his body relaxed in defeat. My eyes locked with his and I knew, as I gazed into them, my state trooper jock was broken!

"Okay...yes just don't send this out!" he begged voice cracking.

"Okay... what?" I pressed!

Mike, the macho stud state trooper, just gazed at me with a whipped look in his green eyes, "okay... SIR!" he responded in a quivering voice.

"Good," I chuckled, "now into the backroom and get bareassed boy!" He cringed on the word "boy" but, like the well-trained cop, he quietly went into the room. When I came in he was naked-his uniform in a heap in the corner. His hands were in front of his crotch-not so "cocky" now I laughed to myself. I reached into my back pocket while he stared at me and pulled out a leather-studded dog collar. I threw it at him. He caught it.

"Put this on dog," I ordered, "want my cop dog collared at all times" He looked at the collar in his hands then at me. I pressed the video button and the "Mikie show" came on again. He heard the first moans and quickly collared himself. Good boy, I thought.

"Now doggie time for your training." I chuckled.

"Training sir?" Mike inquired in a voice that betrayed his concern.

"Don't you ever question me dog," I yelled, "or that tape goes to your captain – got it."

"Yes sir," he said now truly scared and whipped.

"Now bark for me pooch!" I growled, "And put something into it, get on all fours and howl for me, now!" He dropped at once on his hands and knees while raising his head to see me, "ARF! ARF! ARF!"

"HOWL! I SAID."

"AHWHOOO. ARF! ARF! AHWHOOOOOOOO," my cop barked.

I could see the veins bulging on his neck as he howled on all fours. The humiliation just poured out of his eyes! I signaled him to stop and crawl over to me. Watching Mike do it gave me a charge. If only the kids from long ago could see their macho stud quarterback now. Dog collared. Barking. And on all fours!

"Now let's see how my good doggie begs," I sneered, "come on Mikie up on your hind quarters".

Mike rose up and opened his mouth. His tongue hung out and he panted for me. As I stared down, I noticed that his cock had gotten semi hard. "Well, Mike I see you get off on this huh?"

Mike looked down in horror, his face flushed. "No...It's not possible...no sir...I can't...I don't understand... "He stammered now totally at sea.

"Never mind doggie," I said in a voice dripping with fake concern as I tousled his hair, "happens all the time."

Mike turned red the flush coming up from that beautiful hairy chest to his cheeks. He was in a total mind fuck zone - just where I wanted him!

"I don't understand." he replied in a choked whisper - staring at his dick, which filled out a bit more.

"Well lets not worry about it for now just get on your back so I can give my cute puppy his belly rub," I replied as I reached down to stoke his rod further. Mike did as he was told, he was in complete confusion both about the stimulation he was feeling and, his agreeability to my comments - both of which were courtesy of the designer drug I had poured down him when I left him this morning. A sort of time delayed version of yesterdays bottled vapors now available in pill form from the lab boys, By my count it was due to go into effect right about now! I began to rub his hard pack, occasionally letting my hands group his crotch for a little extra fun. As I fondled my cop's jewels, it stiffened a bit more and a sigh escaped from his lips. I began to caress his tits, tickling the hairs just enough to get him squirming. In a few minutes each nipple was hard and stiff. When I looked at Mike, his eyes were closed and his chest was moving in a slow up and down rhyme. I concentrated on massaging his rising pecker and noticed that his pelvis rose up pressing his cock harder against my hands. I massaged him more and his eyes opened - those green beacons now clouded in heavy lidded sexual heat! "Good doggie," I muttered as I rubbed his dick and bull sack, "Does my doggie like it?" I teased as I fondled him.

"AAAHHH Whoof, Whoof," came his low moans.

"Well let's try something else shall we," I purred, "turn over Mikie and let's give you a cleaning okay. Get on all fours again." Mike complied at once while I continued feeling him up. I reached over to the nearby table for that "special something" I had purchased recently. "Spread those hind legs for your master doggie." I said softly. Mike was so turned on by now he never questioned, just obeyed. He spread his muscular legs exposing that cherry chute of his to my view. I examed every curly hair around that untouched, for now, flower. His asshole was moist and beckoning. It seemed to wink at me in longing. I couldn't disappoint it I thought, that would be criminal. Gently I applied lubricants to the entrance as I continued stroking him. He lowered his head into his arms forming a sort of pyramid with his butt as the peak and let out a sigh. It was then I inserted the nozzle of the super large enema bag I had ordered.

"Now you behave okay while I clean you out Mikie," I stated as I released the warm water into his butt hole.

Mike stiffened and his head rose up "Oh god!" he said trying to move forward but, as he did, so did I! The nozzle stayed tight in him.

"Take it Mike or else," I reminded him. That did the trick as he stayed still while I filled him up.

"Oh man it starting to hurt," he moaned as the bag emptied its contents into him.

I watched, noticing that the ridges of his six-pack started to fill out as his insides filled up with the liquid. He moaned more but kept taking it. After a bit his stomach got round with the beginnings of a paunch. I cut off the flow and had him stand up.

"Nice. Yes nice." I stated as I rubbed his now engorged tummy feeling the soft give it had with one hand while I stroked Mike's semi-hard cock with the other.

"Please sir," he cried, his lips quivering with beaded sweat on the upper lids, "Please I need to go bad sir." His eyes were tearing. I gave him a sympathetic look, "well, your master is not cruel. You may go to the bathroom over there; when you finish then shower yourself as well, and return." He started to walk quickly from me. "Now, is that the way my doggie supposed to walk," I stated in a firm voice. Mike stopped, looked back at my frowning face, and knew what I meant; he got down on all fours and crawled slowly to the bathroom – his stomach hanging low between his arms and legs all filled to its capacity. As he left, I called out to him. "Now that's a good, obedient pooch!" I waited planning my next move. After all a wink should never be ignored!

Part Three

I listened to the shower running and quickly got undressed. After a few more minutes, Mike came out still toweling his head dry. As he looked up, he saw me on the bed, my eyes examining his body. A flush came to his cheeks and I found myself getting hard just looking at him. He was like a sculpted Greek statue. I patted to the empty place next to me on the bed, "up here doggie." Mike, still wearing his collar I observed, dropped his towel and onto all fours and lumbered up to the bed. Yeah, I thought he was training up great! As he climbed in his cock flopped around in a flaccid but still impressive state. "Did you masturbate in that shower "I asked harshly? Mike turned red. I had my answer but pressed the point. "WELL! " I shouted.

"Yeesss sir..." he wailed, "but I...It was... I mean while I was scabbing...I..." his voice breaking into a kid's whine that satisfied me even more than his embarrassment.

"Bad dog." I replied swatting his rump in displeasure. Mike took it in silence head bowed in misery.

"Alright then, on your back now! Eyes shut." I commanded secretly taking my bottle from the drawer next to the bed after he had complied. I put the bottle by his nose. He recognized it and stopped breathing to avoid inhaling but I landed a solid punch into his stomach to correct that fast!

"Oof," he cried as the air left him. It was so unexpected that he wasn't prepared and he inhaled in a reflex action to suck in air – only the "air" was pure bottle vapors!

"Oh god", he cried as the vapors effects kicked it, "no...oh shit..." his speech getting more slurred. I pressed the bottle closer letting him suck more in. His eyes opened with that now familiar glaze while his mouth formed that goofy grin. I reached over to stroke him into arousal as he closed his eyes and let out a long sigh. Smiling to myself, I began to caress his balls, watching as they hardened and grew tight. My fingers slipped behind them to that soft moist spot where his sack met his ass. Final count down Trooper Mike my boy I thought as I ran my fingers across the crack of his butt! I moved on top of Mike, our bodies touching, the feel of his body under mine, the tickling of his chest hairs on my skin. Mike's eyes opened into mine and I found myself falling into that green sea of his. Lowering my mouth, I touched his lips. They parted and the next thing I knew, our tongues were exploring deep inside each other's throats. I'll say this, good old Mike was some hot kisser. I was tempted to linger there for hours just kissing but I had a date with a "wink." I broke off, began a slow descent from his mouth, down his throat, over his now firm aroused tits and, down his pack tasting every part of his skin in a series of kisses and nips that had my dog cop moaning up a storm and his dick leaking a steady stream.

"YEAH...oh fucking yeah!" Mike growled, his body quivering and squirming under my tongue's assault!

"Like it doggie," I asked half in jest. "I can stop Officer."

"Oh dam noooo..." Mike replied, "don't...please...ahhhhh yeah." He was grinding his body against mine so hard I could feel every muscle in my stud.

I got to his cock and started to lick the head slit watching while it reddened and expanded in my grasp. By now Mike was groaning in heat gazing at me in heavy lidded eyes of mounting sexual frenzy. My tongue traveled down his now erect pole savoring the texture of his cock with its throbbing veins till, at last, I reached his balls. I licked each one twisting the hairs on his skin gently, and then I sucked them both in my mouth rolling them, pulling them, getting my trooper's man spheres hot, moist, and primed!

"Damm..." he screamed, "oh damm...that's...shit I'm so turned on sir..." he gasped. " Suck my balls...oh fuck...never knew it was so freaking hot."

I sucked faster pulling them down low in my throat. Mike's voice filled the room as he thrust his waist up to the air. I had my opening and I took it. I released his balls from my mouth and ran my tongue down that warm soft spot behind them. Reaching up I grabbed each of his muscular thighs and spread them wide. There was that sly winking chute. In a second, I was on it giving Mike his first rimming! The effect on him was electric.

"AAAAHHHH...shhhhiiiitttt... sir..." he whailed. "Don't stop...no one's ever touched me there!"

I continued my assault pressing in deeper. Going to open him up. Deeper I said to myself feeling the bed shaking as Mike bucked on it. I pushed his thighs farther apart and went in more with my tongue. His asshole muscles began to spasm and then...I was in! My tongue felt the sides of his inner ass. The goal was in sight.

"Deeper...please sir deeper..." cried Mike.

"You sure you want it pooch?" I replied.

"YES SIR! AAAWHOOO..." he howled now totally turned on to it all. Well, how could I refuse? I reached to the table for lube and, after giving Mikie another hit of the bottle, applied a nice glob of lube to his waiting butt hole. As my finger went in Mike groaned. When I hit his prostate I thought he'd hit the ceiling. His cock was like a running jis stream by now and he was sailing fast. I knew it was now!

"Open up," I whispered as my dick pressed at his hole. Mike gasped as I pressed in.

"Jesus nooooo..." he whimpered, "no one's ever...oh shit..."

He started to move but I grabbed onto his thighs and drove in hard.

"AAAAAAA...OOOOHHHHHHH...my asssssssss!" Mike cried.

I fucked harder oblivious to my trooper's pleas. With each thrust I felt my victory complete. I was riding my stallion to the finish line and it was then I realized that Mike was starting to get into it. I felt his hips bucking in rhyme to my strides. He was turned on to it all! I heard his protests changing in mid fuck to pleas for more!

"OH yeah fuck me...fuck me...I love it sir...Take my cop straight asssss!" He moaned as I pumped faster turned on to the knowledge that my stallion had been fucked into a brood mare! I reached down to stroke his cock and, as I did, I felt his ass muscles clamp in a spasm. All at once, Mike erupted, his cock shooting a geyser of juice up like a volcano. As he did, I came as well filling his cop's hole with my searing hot cum, branding his cherry walls with my mark! When I withdrew, Mike let out a long breath.

"More sir..." he whimpered, "Please fuck me more sir."

I laughed, "Don't worry I intend to!" slapping his butt for emphasis. For the rest of the night I screwed and mouth fucked Mike every which way. He moaned, begged, barked, and whimpered for joy every moment. A marathon session had me exhausted by morning. When dawn broke, I had gotten my revenge in full complete with video tape from the cameras I had secreted in the room. With a little judicious face/voice, alterations to conceal my identity the tapes would be ready for shipment to everyone in our high school class in time for the upcoming reunion. I gazed at Mike sleeping in his dog collar sucking a cum smeared thumb. Oh, the next reunion would be a real howler for state trooper and former star stud quarterback Mike... "AHHWHOOOO!"

MY BROTHER'S KEEPER

Part One

It's always tough being the 'younger brother' but in my case, it was pure hell. You see Sean was a natural athlete who easily excelled at any sport he tried. He was also possessed the type of body they used as a model for those Greek sculptures you see in museums. Combine that with killer green eyes, light blonde hair and that Abercrombie and Fitch handsomeness. Well you do the math here.

Me? Well I'm no slouch but I stink in sports. I'm okay body wise. I mean I swim and work out but I'm just average in looks and just make 5'8". Sean is the golden boy and he's known that since we were kids. His ego easily fills his 6'2" frame and he delights in running my life. Trouble is we are opposites in everything. I like to study; he barely knows there is such a thing as a schoolbook. I am a computer whiz while he can barely turn it on. I give way in things; he bullies his way into getting what and whomever he wants. Our major difference however is that Sean is relentlessly straight. He has been deflowering girls since early on. Now at 19 and a High School senior, his sexual prowess and technique are legendary. Me, well I'm 18, still a virgin and well, totally gay in my desires. In fact, my major desires run into two areas. First, taking Sean down from his perch and two...ok I'm admitting it... taking Sean sexually. Hey, the guy's a total wet dream even if he is my brother okay!

Well, one day I caught a break. I was at the library doing research for one of Sean's psych papers (Sean was spending that Sat. afternoon playing at a high school football game for the adoring crowds - did I mention he was captain of the freaking football, wrestling, and baseball teams?).

Anyway it was my job, if I valued my health of course, to do the research and type the paper since later that night Sean was going to be to busy with his next 'game'. Seems he was planning a 'deflowering' after the football game with this cheerleader he'd been cruising from the opposing team. How did he put it, oh yeah, "Going to let that bitch slobber over my 8" uncut man-meat and give her throat a real treat!"

Yeah he thought the rime was the bomb! Sad part was I was envying that poor girl her future snack. Real pathetic huh?

Now where was I, oh right. I was pulling down some books and came across one that dealt with mind control. I don't know why but I opened the book and started reading. After a few minutes it hit me and I suddenly found the solution to my desires. I would mentally cold-conk my brother's brain and convert my raging bull alpha male jock brother into a submissive docile heifer!

Part Two:
Operation Launch

I spend the next two weeks studying that book's techniques as well as other books in the library on that subject. The following two weeks were spent preparing Sean a 'special' porno tape to help me win 'my man'!

Our parents were scheduled to go away for a long delayed two-week vacation and I figured that was the best time to launch "Operation Gelding the Stallion"! The first night they were away, I knew Sean had plans to fuck his latest prey. I also knew that he had been revved up for it for the better part of the week. Knowing my oversexed brother, I knew that by that night his hormones would be in full overdrive. I simply called the 'prey' early on Sat. and cancelled the date for him without his knowledge then casually told him just before he was to leave for it. Our conversation at that point went something like this:

"Oh bro, fuck...I forgot...yeah I'm an ass...no, I think it was some infection she had... yeah real bitch huh...hey, lets get off on a tape I just got...no sorry I meant just you...but bro let me set you up!

I put in the tape, poured him a beer, and watched from the next room as brother Sean played the prepared tape. I had implanted a low visual signal in the tape that induced a hypnotic trance in the subject. All it needed was the intense concentration of the viewer over a short time period. The porno scenes provided that for me. If you figured in the sexual stimulations to Sean's brain combined with the tranquilizing effects of the alcohol big brother never had a chance.

I watched as Sean stroked his meat. He was really into the tape and it was hot watching big brother working his cock. He was breathing hot and heavy and at one point he slipped his free hand up his shirt giving me a fantastic view of his six-pack and quarter sized nipples. He played with one nipple then the other till each one got hard. Yeah, the nipples weren't the only thing that rose right about then either. This was better than seeing any tape but I had to wonder if anything was going to happen. Then it did! Slowly Sean's hand job slowed as well as his breathing, which had been pretty heavy before. Soon his breathing slowed into a steady rhyme. I noticed his eyelids flutter then droop in stages till they closed. By the end of the tape, my jock stud muffin was out of it but good. I walked over to him.

I gazed down at my zonked older brother sitting there his face relaxed, a peaceful look on his handsome face, and his hand still gripping his flaccid cock. If the program worked, his inner psyche was ready to absorb anything I said to him. Time to start his reprogramming. I bent close and whispered into his hopefully receptive mind. If I had any qualms about what I was going to do, being that close to him and picking up the sexy scent he was giving off just then killed them.

"Sean...you there bro," I inquired attentively.

"Yes," he weakly replied.

"Sean," I said with fingers crossed. "You must listen to me and obey everything I tell you."

"Listen and obey," he nodded.

So far so good then, I thought, "Sean, open your eyes." Slowly he did and I saw his killer greens were glazed and unfocused. I was in!

"Sean, repeat after me, I'm a fuck up."

"You are a fuck up," he responded. Ghees I'd have to be more precise I realized.

"No Sean...YOU are the fuck up." I stated sternly.

His eyes blinked and after a hesitation he said, "I'm...am...a..." then he paused. His ego was fighting me!

"SEAN," I barked roughly, "YOU ARE A FUCK UP!"

"I...amm...no...no," he protested calmly. Dam he was smug!

"Sean you are a fuck up," I insisted.

I could see his brain processing it trying to resist it. I needed to divert his brain's resistance, something to deflect his concentration. I gazed at him just lying there with his cock hanging out. That was it! I reached down and began to stoke his meat. It felt firm and warm. I ran my hand across his pole enjoying the feel of its heft and length. True to form, my sexually overcharged brother responded at once with a boner. As his breathing quickened I leaned in close and whispered firmly. "Sean you are a fuck up!" I increased my strokes reveling in the touch of his thick hard cock.

"I...oh shit," he moaned as I quickened my pump on his meat turning up the sexual heat. I felt a surge of power course through me. For the first time big jock stud boy was helpless against me. I had his manhood in my grip and, more importantly, had him physically squirming. Time to break his mind now.

"Give it up Sean," I encouraged as I increased my rhyme. "You are a fuck up."

"I...am..." he was fighting but I had the upper hand now so to speak. I continued my assault.

"Fuck up...you are a fuck up," I insisted as I raced to the finish line. I felt his cock grew rock hard in my grip. I ran my palm up and down enjoying the throb of his veins as the blood pulsated in his engorged warrior. I could see his pupils spinning and beads of sweat breaking out on his upper lips. He was turned on big time. "You are a fuck up. You are a fuck up." I chanted with each stroke as I drove the thought home by letting it ride in on a sexual highway to his control centers. His mind could concentrate on either resisting or on getting off. Knowing super-stud I figured the latter had the home field advantage.

"I... fuck up...me...oh fuck..." he babbled as his hormones raged in his brain. Which door... the old' the lady and the tiger' plot. His brain chose! "I...fuck up...yes? "

I was almost there. I ordered him to repeat it to me again even as I continued jerking jock boy off. Sean's cock lurched in my hands. He was getting ready to blow his wad.

"Admit you are a fuck up and you can cum," I yelled. He whimpered and then, it happened. He just lost it!

"I'M A FUCK-UP... A FUCK UP... A FUCK UP...AAAAAA...AHH." Touchdown!

Sean roared as he erupted surrendering to both that idea and his sexual needs. He shot his load in a giant arch that splattered over his chest and pants. Had to admit that big brother's climax was impressive. I leaned back and took in the sight. Sean lay panting on the chair trying to suck in air. He had suffered his first defeat at my hands! My first win but not the entire game yet. "Sean, you need your little brother to run things before you fuck up more." I stated calmly.

"Yeah need my little brother's help." He nodded dully.

"It turns you on to listen to him," I suggested as I again rubbed his cock. Sean hardened once more and his mouth curled up in a smile. "Listening to him is a turn on," he muttered agreeably.

"He is your idol. Obeying him is what you want!" I insisted as I gave his meat further manual stimulations.

"Oh...fuck," he gasped as he wiggled under my renewed hand job. Sean's constant desire to get off coupled with that initial admission of submission had rendered him pliable now. "My idol...fuck yeah...

need to please him yeah!" Now that was getting somewhere I mused as he groaned in my grip.

For the next three hours, using a combination of suggestions for his future submissiveness coupled with some continued hand jobs on my zonked brother I was able to set up some basic reprogramming in him. By the end of the first session, I'd accomplished two things: first, I'd trained Sean to be my devoted servant and, two; I'd milked my stud-muffin dry.

"Last time, tell me again," I inquired as I masturbated my brother for the final time that night. I wanted to make sure that I had him and hell, the rush of my power over him at last was still exciting. Holding that stud meat in my grip while he groveled under my touch was intoxicating!

"I'm a complete fuck up," he babbled while his body squirmed under my sexual ministrations. My cocky arrogant big brother wasn't so cocky now. The room was filled with his painful gasps and whimpers as he struggled to cum again. "My little brother is my boss. It turns me on to submit to him. Ahh shittt...ohhh...fucccccc...!" His body went rigid as he climaxed. I laughed as I saw a pathetic dribble emerge from his rod. He sighed and went limp in the chair. Jock boy had been sexually taken down and totally spent. His dick had been drained! I had won another round. I went to bed leaving my stallion sitting in the chair his front pants and upper body soaked in jis. Like they said in that old movie whose name, I forget. "Tomorrow is another day!"

Part Three:
Oh What a Beautiful Morning!

The next day I woke up and raced downstairs. There was Sean dead to the world, lying there in cum stained pants and chest, his impressive meat flaccid and obviously cum stuck to the front of his fly. Well, I couldn't ask for a better scene to see if last nights brain molding had taken firm root.

"What the hell is this shit?" I roared, making sure I looked annoyed.

"Huh...what," my humpy brother muttered as he woke up. He shook his head as if he was trying to clear up his mind then focused on me and followed my gaze to his crotch. "Oh shit." He said as his face flushed red.

"Are you that much of a loser?" I barked. "You jerk-off all night and fall asleep in your own jis?"

Sean's eyes met mine. After a second of anxiety by myself, I heard music to my ears.

"I'm... sorry bro...I'm... please...I fucked up again," his voice drifted off weakly. I had done it. I'd short- circuited the self-confident arrogant bastard!

"It's alright bro," I oozed in fake concern as I reached over to rub his head like I'd do with a child. "Little brother will fix it all up."

Sean broke out in a smile of gratitude and adoration. I noticed his cock stir slightly. He must have felt it as well because another blush came to his cheeks. "I'll go shower," he mumbled quickly as he pushed his now semi-hard cock into his pants.

"You do that Sean," I smiled, "then after you clean up we will talk about what I expect from you while mom and dad are away. After all, I'm in charge right?"

"Yes sir," he replied. "You are definitely in charge!" I saw his cock stiffen further in his pants as he said that. Yes, things were looking up!

I watched as he got out of the chair and climbed the stairs. His hard bubble jock butt was outlined in his tight pants. Hmmm, I thought. "Sean," I called out to him. He turned. "After you shower I think we will do some cherry picking." I laughed. "That okay with you?"

"Whatever you say bro," he smiled a bit confused. "You the one in charge!"

My Brother's Keeper II

Part One:
Field Of Dreams

It had been three days since I first 'sacked' my brother with a hypnotic zinger to his control centers. Three fun filled days of watching my formerly arrogant tormentor bend over backwards to please me and, judging from the boner he sprouted when he did so (courtesy of my hypnotic command to him), pleasing himself in the bargain. Should I mention that for some reason he found that, for the first time since he sprouted crotch hairs, he couldn't, unless he knew he was pleasing me, get a hard-on or let alone cum during those three days. I wonder what put that thought in his brain huh - hehehe. Until now, I doubt super-stud Sean had ever had a day he had not gotten his rocks off. I listened by his bedroom door as he tried every night, without success, to get 'old faithful' to gush. The sound of slapping skin coupled with groans of despair and frustration was the bomb. By the third day, my ever-ready bunny was suffering a bad case of blue balls and was ready to erupt! It was time to move to the next step in my operation.

"Hey Sean," I said casually on the third night after he had come home early from his date. From the look on his face, the guy had just had another incomplete play! "Bro, you appear upset, anything wrong?"

He glanced up at me. His handsome face a study in conflict on whether to tell me his dilemma. Ah, the humiliation he'd experience would be great. But little did he suspect it was just his first taste of that cup.

"No... its just," he flushed as he tried to get it out.

"Sean," I said in my most brotherly tone, "trust me bro. Come on I enjoy helping you." Bingo, the magic words to Sean's brain. Please me and you get aroused. Sure enough, his helmeted warrior sprung to life. I gazed at it and noticed Sean noticing my gaze. He turned scarlet!

"I can... why now... never... oh shit," he moaned pathetically. "Why with a guy... shit my own brother too." His voice drifted off

"Sean," I stated paternalistically, "I understand bro. Hey you've been under stress that's all. It's nothing man."

"You think?" he muttered seeking any excuse to explain his arousal.

"Bro, you just got to believe man." I replied with a fake knowing tone, "Just stress from the game dude. You are not popping rods with any other guys are you?"

"Fuck no way man," he quickly retorted. "Just you." He slipped it out before he knew what he was saying. On hearing himself, say it his face went red once more.

"Sean," I sighed as I took his hand in sympathy. God I was good! "You got another big game for the weekend. You mind is stressed so that's why you...ahem." Sean stared at me drinking it up like mother's milk. At this point, any explanation made sense to him.

"But why with you?" he asked miserably.

"Cause with me you know you are safe bro," I lectured with a smile,

"You know I take care of you so...no stress...plus delayed reactions to your date tonight...see."

"Yeah I do," my jock stud toy nodded. God he was easy.

"Tell you what brother. Let me set you up with another tape and you'll see things will return to normal alright." I suggested

"That would be great," he gushed, "yeah set me up man." He broke into a grin. Oh, brother hope you remember you did after all ask to be set up.

That night I 'set up' my big brother with another 'specially prepared' porno tape to watch. The poor hunk thanked me repeatedly and barely was able to cover his man meat's arousal until I left the room. Of course I managed to observe the 'show' from a side window and sure enough had the fun of seeing my hunk stroke his cock to an impressive size only to sink into a trance before he had reached a climax. I reentered the room. Although there was probably no need to I reached down to fondle his cock into arousal. Hey no need to tinker with success right.

"Sean you hear me," I asked quietly as I felt his cock grow in my grip. Damn the power I felt as I wakened my older brother's manhood.

"Yeth," he muttered. His hard body wiggled as his rod rose to full glory. He let out a sexy growl. His hips rose up slightly as he began to push his dick through my grip. The horny bastard was fucking my palm. Shit it was a hot! I could feel his foreskin slipping through my grasp. His breathing deepened and his chest expanded pushing so tight against his shirt that I could make out his hard nipples. He was turned on big time Yep; big brother's brain was ready to receive my next toss of the game ball.

"Sean, you get off on sex don't you," I asked sure of the answer.

"Fuck yessss," he hissed as he began to thrust his pelvis up and down using my hand like it was some poor girl's hole. Sean in fucking mode was sexy all right.

"Sean, remember you get off even more when you please me right." I insisted as I picked up my pump on his cock to help him out.

"Getting off cause you are pleased," he moaned as his hips drove up from the chair.

"Remember you are turned on when I'm pleased with you." I intoned again as I jerked his cock to a finish.

"Turned on... So fucking turned on!" He cried as he thrust up and down faster. His shirt was drenched in sweat showing off his tightly defined muscular body and especially his six-pack.

"Remember, that Sean. You are turned on when I'm pleased with you." I pumped him faster.

Sean nodded furiously and then he let out a strangled cry. At that second, he rammed his hips up and I felt his jis flood in his cock and then, blow out in a spray of creamy white.

"FUCK... PLEASE MY BROTHER...TURN ON..." Sean roared as he sent forth wave after wave of his pent up jis. He lay in the chair. His cock, chest, and pants soaked in white suds and an angelic smile on his face. I whispered some instructions to him then, left him. I figured he could use the rest. Hey tomorrow was a big game and my playbook was set for it!

A Boner Book

Part Two:
What Comes Up

It was an important game. Everyone was there including me. I rarely went to see Sean play but hell; you got to support your man right.

The team came onto the field and when the crowd saw Sean, they erupted in screams. He was, after all, the golden boy. I saw him glance into the stands as he came onto the field trying to find me. I waved down and gave him a high sign. A beautiful smile came to his face and an impressive boner rose in his uniform tights. You couldn't help noticing that rise in his athletic cup as it strained to break through his pants. A few girls in the cheerleader squad started to giggle and then a murmur came up from the crowd. I could see the panic in big jock bro's eyes as he tried to cover it with his helmet. He gazed up, our eyes locked and, I gave him the thumbs up. He swayed slightly and then dropped the helmet. Yep he was under as per a hypnotically induced command I had given him before he left that morning. He stood there in front of the home crowd with his hard-on showing as it pressed against his uniform pants. He began to rub it as people squealed in shock or glee. The coach noticed the buzz going on, Sean standing there before the crowd dumbstruck, rubbing his crotch in front of everyone, and then that boner! He went up to Sean and started yelling. Getting no response, he grabbed him and shook him. Sean snapped out of it. Saw his 'mound' and appeared to be babbling in panic as the coach gestured at him. It was clear to everyone that the coach was tearing 'golden boy' a new ass. It was a red-faced Sean that went on the field to the now mocking crowd!

"Hey Sean what's UP!" hooted some guys in the crowd. By now everyone was laughing. Soon the opposition took up the cheer!

"What's up Doc? What's up Doc?" They retorted with that famous line. It was with some amusement I observed my arrogant athlete get his first critical reviews. For the rest of the game two things were clear. Sean's timing and play were way off and at various moments during the game he would, after seeing me give a high sign, sprout another boner. At last, the coach decided to bench him. Sean had never had that happen before and it was a truly demoralized stud that left the field.

I slipped down to meet him in the tunnel to the lockers just walking on air. Just before I arrived, however Sean met up with his best friend Brent who was our school's star soccer, swimmer, and track athlete. Brent had a finely cut muscled body. At just 6 feet with wavy black hair, blue eyes, and highly sensual facial features he was, next to Sean of course, one fine piece of meat as many ladies in town could testify. I moved back to keep out of sight but within hearing range.

"Sean what the fuck is going on," Brent yelled. "Fucking up like that on the field. Sporting hard-ons in front of everyone."

"I'm...I..." sobbed Sean his voice cracking.

"Don't go all faggy on me bud." Brent replied in annoyance at Sean's display of emotion. "Christ you sound like that pussy brother of yours now."

At that, Sean's head shot up. He grabbed Brent's shirt. "Don't insult my brother you bastard," he growled.

"Easy bro, easy okay," Brent replied coolly. "Listen Sean just get it together okay."

Sean released his grip and, with his head down walked back to the lockers. Brent watched him go shaking his head. "Damn I think that family has got two pussies now!" Brent muttered out of Sean's hearing but not mine. He turned to walk back into the stands. I stared in anger and, okay, some lust–hell his butt in those tight jeans were owwwee! Yet, someplace in my brain his name was checked off. I went to find my demoralized brother. Time to get him home for some fun. Brent was a future issue for now!

Part Three:
Bro, It's all in the Proteins

It was a silent Sean that I drove home from the game. I let him alone during the drive to allow him to fully process his ego's destruction. Benched and laughed off his field of glory. It was low ebb for him and the perfect time to put the final nail in my alpha boy stud. By tomorrow morning, the family's big raging stallion would be gelded to become my own passive brood mare.

We walked silently in and Sean went into his room mumbling something about changing then going to the basement to workout. Dad had set up a separate weight room down there and Sean went there everyday to keep in shape. At other times, he just went there to 'chill'. I guess chilling was in order all things considered. I set up a tape and then went to his bedroom door and knocked. "Sean come out here and talk with me." I said in mock sympathetic tones. I heard a shuffle and the door opened. Sean was standing there, eyes downcast, and he had changed into his workout sweats. He looked like one of those gay pix you see in the magazines. He had on a tight gray cotton shirt that was two sizes too small showing off his defined chest, tapered narrow waist and well cut abs. Sean always wore these blue satin shorts that clung to his bubble butt and emphasized his hefty cock and sack. Pure animal sexuality and soon to be all mine.

"Sean, come here I said as I opened my arms to hug him." Am I good or what.

Sean moved forward and I felt his hard muscled body in my grip. I savored the sensuality of the contact then released him and looked into his green eyes. "Listen dude you had an off day. You've been tense all week that's all. Fuck 'em okay. Just know I'm always pleased with you!" I insisted as I gently brushed my fingers through his light blonde hair. Sean gazed at me in pure adoration and, since we still touching below the waist, I was treated to a nice firm hard-on by my hypno-zonked boy.

"Before you go workout I think you need to relax with this tape I just got. It's especially for you as a present and no it's not porno." I chuckled. "Just an artistic swirl of relaxing colors. I was told all the big sports stars use it to clear their minds."

"Really." Sean said in a husky voice. Poor bro was overcome with emotion as my consideration.

"Nothing is too good for our golden boy." I smiled as I swung my arm around his waist and guided him to his chair. On the way, I casually dropped my hand to his ass and ran my palm across the hard blue satin package under it. I felt the stirring of lust in my own body. Soon. Very soon. I popped in the tape and left him to watch it. I had prepared a hypnotic trance program under images of complex shifting colors. This time I let the whole tape play. By its end, Sean's brain would be permanently programmed to accept my rewiring.

Sean lay in the chair with eyes glazed. Time to pop open his brain and do some rewiring I mused.

"Sean," I said quietly. "You hear me?"

"Yeses," he sighed.

"You are one royal fuck-up huh," I queried.

"Yes," my hypno-conked stud muffin agreed. Today's disaster had only cemented that belief in his brain. Just, what I had intended when I set him up for it.

"You need your little brother to get it right." I suggested

"Need him. Badly...yeah," jock-boy acknowledged.

"Sean," I stated calmly, "You get turned on by your brother big time don't you?"

"I get turned on by my brother...yes," he admitted. Even zapped he blushed at the admission.

I reached under the waistband of his satin shorts and began to massage his basket. The cool feel of the satin on one side of my hand with the moist hard ribbed supporter rising against the other side was intoxicating. My dick hardened fast! Hang on I mentally sent word to it. Relief is coming!

"He turns you on huh?" I teased.

"Yesssss," my football hunk gasped as his crotch thrust up to rub my palm. Sure enough, my muscle god was in fuck mode once more. His narrow waist bounced up and down as he tried to screw my palm.

"OOOHHHHHFUUUC..." he growled as his waist moved in rapid piston-like motions in the chair.

"You want his body in you Sean." I stated. "You need his body!"

"Want...brother's body." Sean repeated. In some inner part of his mind, a lone fort of his former psyche held out for a short while but then the last defenders of his straightness succumbed to his overwhelming sexual drive. He was too zapped after all these tapes and the sexual stimulations to fight it now successfully. The last remnant of that macho girl-fucking arrogant jock stud was tackled and gelded. In the ashes would rise his new role: BOTTOMBOY!

"You need him sexually," I chanted to him, "You need his body, want it in you, taste it, desire it, have to have it!"

"FUCKING NEED MY BROTHER'S BODY...FUCKING NEED IT IN ME...YEAH" he screamed as his new programming broke out in full flower and his cock exploded in his supporter.

I withdrew my hand and went to get a washcloth. Gently I ordered him to stand up then; I striped off his shorts and supporter and cleaned my big brother off like he was a baby. I slipped a new jockstrap on him and, then his shorts. His muscular legs were a major turn on to my touch as well but I held off.

"You need to taste his juices Sean," I gleefully instructed. "Getting his protein in you will make you a better athlete."

"Juices... better athlete." He agreed.

"Drink his juices everyday and you will be a good athlete and stop fucking up." I teased.

"Drink his spunk. Never fuck up. Better athlete." Sean's brain processed.

"You asshole tingles to have him fuck you as well," I insisted.

"My asshole needs him." Sean accepted quickly. He was mentally an open glass waiting to be filled. One I intended to fill before I ahem, filled the rest of him!

"You're wet down there for him!" I laughed enjoying his submission and degradation.

"Fucking wet," he repeated as his butt clenched and flexed with its newfound hunger.

"Girls don't interest you sexually now. Only guys. Sexually servicing your brother and any guy he tells you too makes you hot!" I commanded as I approached the goal line.

"Servicing my brother and whomever he tells me too makes me hot." Sean groaned as his hand reached down to stroke his meat. It stiffened rapidly. Yes, he was there. Time to cash in now.

"Sean after a few minutes you will awake refreshed, happy, and with a need to seduce your brother," I implanted into my willing receptacle.

"Seduce him... fuck yeah." Sean muttered.

"Invite him to work out with you Sean." I suggested. "Then seduce him there."

"Hmmmm, fuck yeah," Sean said sexily.

Game time! I shook Sean. He woke with a start. "Wow I must have drifted off there bro," he laughed. "Hey lets hit the workout bench downstairs okay?"

"Fine you start I'll be there in a bit." Sean nodded and went down. He moved with natural grace. He was fucking sexy in those clothes. I scrambled to get changed and went downstairs.

Part Four:
Workout Obsessions

Sean was hard at work lying on the bench doing a rapid series of presses. The room was filled with his sexy sweaty scent. Seeing him there draped across the bench, firm hard legs fixed on the ground, taunt bulging arm muscles flexing as he lifted and, that impressive basket rising as his waist lifted slightly off the bench with each lift sent my hormones into a feeding frenzy. Feeding time's coming guys, I whispered silently to them!

"Hey bro let me spot you." I said as I straddled the bench. I made sure that my legs were positioned on either side of his head and my crotch was directly over his face. Sean's arms shook. By now, my crotch's scent must be filling up his lungs. "You seem to be a bit tired there bro, let me help you get that bar back in its supports alright."

"Thanks," he croaked softly. I noticed that his chest was rising and falling. The only sound in the basement now was Sean's breathing. Big brother was sniffing his first man - odor; judging by the rise in his dick down there the experience was pretty good for him.

I let him enjoy it for a few seconds more as I helped to lower the bar in its slots. As I did, I bent my knees so that my crotch was now slightly touching the tip of his nose. I could feel the warm currents coming from deep in his lungs as I enfolded him in my scent. Just his mouth and upper lip was visible to my downward glance. Sean was licking his lips hungrily. He was going for it.

"Oh fuck," he sighed as his hands reached up to grip my waist and pulls me down onto his face. Electrical sparks set off as my big brother, old arrogant Mr. Straight Stud himself, meekly buried his face in my basket.

"Ommmph," he sounded as he rubbed under me licking through my shorts, and then attacking each inner thigh while his hands pulled at my cotton briefs. I pulled off him and stepped back. His lust filled eyes tried to focus on me. "Please bro," he begged, "need it so bad!"

"I know babe," I hissed. I slipped off my shorts freeing my engorged cock and positioned his head so it dangled just off the bench. Quietly I moved my dick to his waiting mouth. "You really want it?" I teased sternly.

"Fuck yessss," he gasped as his mouth opened and his tongue flicked the head of my rod.

"Take it you cunt." I snarled feeling my victory. I could hear my own cheering crowds as I slide my rod across his tongue and slipped my meat down his eager throat. The touch of his hot mouth tongue guided me into deep into him as my formerly heterosexual hunk began his first male blowjob.

"Ummmpphh," he gurgled as he sucked me off in a sexual frenzy.

"Yeah slurp it in bro," I howled as I face fucked him. "Drink it down you arrogant bitch." I felt the inferno of his mouth slurping away on my rod as the sucking sounds of my new pussy-boy filled the weight room. Glancing down I could see Sean's hands down his blue distended satin shorts beating his man meat. If his friends could see the golden boy now I thought. The big tough athletic hero lying on his back giving head to his own brother and turned-on like some pathetic dog in heat while doing it! This was true victory.

I reached down, making sure that my cock remained deep in his mouth, and grabbed each of Sean's legs. I pulled them back and up till pussy-boy was bent up in such a way that his body was resting on his shoulders. Quickly I pulled off his satin blues and spread his powerful thighs apart. Sean never stopped sucking or jerking off his meat. Say, what you want my new pussy-boy was single minded.

As his butt hole was exposed part of my brain echoed with the barely whispered opening words from Citizen Kane...rosebud!

I stared at his cute moist pink chute light wet blonde hairs stuck to the ring. I wet a finger and rubbed the outer muscles of his cherry hole. The result was fantastic. My hunk increased both his tongue job on my cock and the hand job on his.

"Oh babe yeah," I uttered, "Get it nice and slick. Taste my precum protein bro." I snarled.

"MMMMMMMMMMM," Sean replied as he sucked on me like a pro.

I inserted a finger in his asshole hit his prostate. His entire body quaked!

A loud groan escaped from Sean's cock filled throat. "FFFFFFFFUUUUUUUUMMMMM."

I preceded to finger fuck him in order to fully open up big brother's virginal entryway. The effect was explosive. Sean began slurping like a mad man. My cock, my ball sack, my inner thighs were his feeding areas. I had to pull off him or risk blowing my wad before it was time.

"Need your juices. Need you in me...oooaaahhh," he implored as I stepped back and walked around him to come up from behind. Sean's head was moving back and forth, his mouth slick with my precum. He had a look of pure bliss no doubt helped along by the masturbation he was giving himself. I straddled the bench, rested each of his sexy legs on each of my shoulders, and put my cock at the castle gate.

"Fuck me," he moaned. "Fuck meeeeee." Big brother was burning up in sexual heat. Time to apply the hose!

I fingered him once more to make sure he was loose. Sean whimpered like the newly created pussy he had become. The old self confident, macho Sean was a thing of the past. It was a new boy under me. Time to brand him as mine. I thrust in!

"AAAARRRRGGGGHHH...FFFFUUUCCCKKK!" My bitch howled as I popped his cherry.

"Take it you bitch," I screamed as I screwed my former stallion. I rode him to glory savoring his silky smooth insides. Soon my boy was thrusting back to literally help my fucking. His man meat was leaking even more cum now. From the redness of its head, it was almost climax time for Sean. I increased my strides in him slapping his ass as I did!

"Oh fuck... you're fucking my ass and slapping it hot toooohhhh." He bellowed.

"Take it you bastard," I roared as I fucked and slapped out a lifetime of humiliation at his hands. My big brother. My tormentor. Now my own cock crazed cunt-boy!

SLAP

SLAP

SLAP

"I'M GOING TO BLOW MY FUCKING SPUNK!" Sean screamed.

His ass muscles suddenly contracted as his dick spewed forth a gallon of hot creamy jis. It hit my chest and its warmth coupled with his chute's contractions sent me over the edge.

"SHIT TAKE MY PROTEIN SHOWER SEAN." I wailed as I seared his insides with my cream. I collapsed onto Sean. We both lay motionless as we came back from the sexual summit we'd been on.

"Fuck...oh fuck," I panted as I looked up to see Sean's face.

He was smiling. He was beautiful. He was mine! The old

resentments were gone. My big brother; my lover.

"I think I need more of that protein sir." He said shyly.

I sat up and took my cock in my hands. Moving up to straddle his chest I guided his waiting mouth onto my newly re-hardened joint. "No problem bro. Here's some more fresh from the spigot!"

Sean slurped me in. Second header coming up!

Part Five:
The Times are a Changing

Well, it's been some time since the launch of my so-called 'gelding operation' and I must say it has all turned out fantastic so far. When our parents returned from vacation, they were surprised by a change in living arrangements. Sean had moved from his own room into mine insisting that he wanted to keep up the close attachment to his 'little brother' that had developed during their absence. End result, mom, and dad now have a free room to use for whatever and Sean gets his 'protein' drink every night all-fresh from the spigot. As for me, hey you do the math!

Sean's grades have improved (hey who wants a dummy for a lover) and he's playing and looking better than ever (well who wants an out of shape one either). Thanks to Sean's help in the weight room, I've developed my own tight buff body too. Tonight, as I write this my bro is doing his nightly tongue bathe on my joint and ball-sack and, to be honest, he looks sexily cute down there sucking merrily away while one of his free hands strokes his own meat to a climax. Okay, yeah I admit it; I find I'm as totally in love with the new Sean as he is with me.

"Hey bro," I teased. "You missed a spot down there." He glanced up with adoration in his eyes and grinned. He is so fucking hot!

"Yes ummmph." He mumbled as slurped my cock some more. God that boy loves his protein drinks!

"When you get done remember my chute needs attention too." I replied as I tousled his hair. We had come a long way. As Sean hit my hole with his moist tongue my mind drifted to thoughts of Brent, the remarks he had made after the game and, my brother's defense of me. "Sean what say we invite good old Brent over for a special movie," I chuckled. Sean just nodded; his mouth was a bit occupied right about then. Yeah-good old Brent. I think it was time for Sean to have his own bottom-boy and Brent to learn the real meaning of the cry of 'GOOALLLLLL'; but first, time to loosen up big brother's other erotic zone. As some now unknown porno star once said in a Matt Sterling video, "Hey bro, let me see dat asssss!"

My Brother's Keeper III: Busting In Brent

Part One:
Jock Daze

It had been a frustrating fall season here in terms of getting Brent hypnotized. After his encounter with my big brother Sean in the stadium after the 'infamous game' (i.e. 'what's up doc') good old Brent had given his 'former best friend' Sean the cold shoulder. There had been no thaw. In fact, their prior friendly competition had taken a decidedly aggressive turn. Getting the 6 ft. stud to the house to see a 'tape' was not going to be easy.

Now you may ask yourself why bother so let me replay some facts for you. Take one muscular jock that letters in soccer, swimming, and track. Combine with sensual looks, wavy curling black hair, and sea-blue eyes. Mix with a severe dash of blue-collar homophobia (Brent's brother, whom Brent idolized, was a big-shot local fireman who boasted how he would make any 'faggot' who applied for a job at the firehouse regret it). Sprinkle with his recent whispering campaign concerning Sean's 'tendencies' among the other school athletes. You get the desire for revenge. Remember, I love new and improved big brother now and Brent's actions led to Sean getting less protection from his teammates when he played football that season. Translation my lover was getting the crap knocked out of him and NO ONE DOES THAT TO MY BROTHER!

Now nailing that bastard was a point of honor yet I'd almost given up hope until a remark from Sean after the close of the football/soccer season. Both Sean and Brent went into another of their respective sports after that. For Sean it was wrestling, for Brent swimming. Key was that unlike football and soccer, which never shared lockers or practice rooms in the gym, these two sports did. Sean mentioned how Brent always mentally prepared alone in the gym by watching swim tapes of the competition and that with a big meet coming up soon he was doing it every night now. Lights went off in my brain.

"Sean can you get the tape Brent will be watching tomorrow?" I asked while we were working out in our weight room (no, not that kind - we work out those muscles later in the bedroom).

"Easy bro. Piece of cake," he huffed as he bench-pressed another higher weight. Big brother was getting his body in shape for wrestling, not that he needed any improvement. Sean lay there on the bench topless, biceps bulging, streaked with a glistening sheen of sweat, and chest muscles straining... damn his body was fine. Watching him lying there on that bench where I had first deflowered him with those luscious brown nipples of his just crying out to be sucked caused a 'muscle' of my own to strain... but time for that later.

So that morning bright and early we slipped into the gym. Sean found the tape and that day I stayed at home doing a bit of implanting. I had just returned it to the file cabinet when I heard the swim team coming in. Luckily, the janitor's closet was open and I was able to slip in.

"Think we got a shot to beat those pansy assed guys in this weekend's competition," boasted a voice I recognized as Brent's. I adjusted the door slits slightly to get a view of the locker room and stepped back to the rear wall to be sure I wasn't seen. The swim team started changing and the scene was one of young hard bodies with ripe asses and hefty baskets on full view.

"Well dude, you're the star here," said a hot looking blonde as he stretched his arms above his head. About 5 ft. 10 inches, well built, nice pac, a cock that was tapered and long and, a tasty set of low hangers; yes, another time man I mused.

"Bet your ass Eric," growled Brent in that husky sexy voice that had quite a number of girls wet with lust whenever he spoke with them. Brent peeled off his suit giving me a great view of his 'assets'. He had a light covering of black hair across his chest that lead downward sensually past his navel to his meat market. An uncut 8-inch pole that was thick and set off by a set of nuts that swung bull-like between two sculpted thighs. When he turned, his bubble butt looked like pure white dimpled marble under the overhead lights. He was powerfully built, cut, and defined. Oh yeah, I nodded to myself. He will be a prize!

"Yeah a good win in this upcoming swim meet will confirm me as the school's top athlete." Brent laughed.

"Aren't you forgetting Sean man?" Asked a striking honey-toned Latino stud. "That guy's a great athlete and he triple letters too."

"That fuck is a pansy assed faggot," yelled Brent hotly. "You saw what happened at that one game of his."

"Man, it was one game," insisted the Latino swimmer. "Besides the dude is a natural on any team he plays. He also is a cool guy..."

"Cool guy huh?" Brent interrupted. "Hey guys," Brent said mockingly, "maybe old Rico is in luvvvvv."

"Fuck you; you bastard," the young Latino muttered. "And the name is Enrico okay. Sean..."

"Sean is a cock-sucker just like his brother. I bet he takes it up the ass too." Brent insisted, as the room got quiet. "Bet he moans like a girl when it happens too. Fuck, my big brother says all faggots moan to get fucked. I'm top dog in this school, got it," he bellowed!

The other swimmers just stared. Brent was the team captain and team star. It was obvious that he ruled the roost. "A lot you know you scumbag," whispered Enrico under his breath so softly that no one but me, and only because he was right by the janitor's door, could hear him.

The team changed and left all except for the humpy blonde Eric and Brent who finished climbing into his team sweats. His manhood's outline pressed up against the tight cotton. Soon; very soon.

"I think you were too hard on Enrico," said Eric who gazed at Brent with undisguised hero worship. No accounting for taste I guess.

"Fuck that spic," Brent snarled, "Only worse thing than having one of 'them' on the team would be having a faggot on it." Brent went over to the cabinet and pulled the tape out. He turned back to Eric," now get out of here. I got some intense mental prep to do." Eric scrambled out and my brother's former 'best friend' went into a side room. I heard the whirl of the VCR. After a few minutes, a long sigh came from the room. I left the closet and crept up to the room's doorway. I glanced in. There he was, dulled eyes locked on the screen, wearing a goofy smile of contentment. Mr. Macho straight star athlete was zapped!

Part Two:
A Swimmer's Strokes

I walked over to my newest conquest careful to avoid getting between Brent and the tape he was watching. I had placed an improved, intensive mind program in it and the effect was evident. Good old Brent showed all the signs of being deeply under. His breathing was slow and rthymic while his pupils were fixed and dilated. I slipped off his sweats to expose his 'family jewels' to easy access. I let the tape play out, rewound it, and then set it on replay. I wanted to be sure that my swim stud was getting a healthy dose of the mind inducing flexibility it contained. He gazed blankly ahead at the screen with a blissfully goofy look on his sensual features. I reached down to fondle his package.

"Oooohhh...yyeeahh," he moaned as I took his impressive testicles in hand.

"Can you hear me Brent?" I whispered leaning close to him. I could smell the mix of chlorine from the pool and the light cologne he wore. Sexy smell all right but I had business to take care of. I continued my interrogation even as I played with his hefty balls. Sean had told me Brent once admitted, in private to him before their friendship ended, that he really got off on ball-play because his nuts were super sensitive. According the Sean the exact quote was, "Dude when some bitch is doing them I blow my fuses so bad I can't even think straight!" Well, time to see if the jock-boy was telling the truth. I could feel the heavy man-juices of my testosterone driven, self proclaimed 'babe-fucker' swirling in them. A thousand little straight warriors all seeking to get out to make baby Brent's. Well, guys not if I can help it. Get ready to be decommissioned!

"You like this?" I asked as I rolled his nuts gently in the palm of my hand. His lightly furry sack tickled seductively. Brent broke out into a grin and his cock answered for him by inflating to a respectable length.

"Fucckk...yeahhh," he gasped as he spread his lean muscular legs apart.

"You get off on this right?" I replied enjoying his movements.

"Hell...oohh mmannnn...big...ahhh...timeeee," he hissed as his body squirmed under my sexual manipulation. I got the same charge of power I initially experienced with Sean before it was replaced by our mutual love. (Okay back to the stud in hand right). That knowledge that a macho, straight, jock stud was quivering like a dog in heat at your manly touch. Then it hit me. That casual remark Brent made before. Well, now hmmm...but that was for later.

"You also get off on swimming don't you?" I inquired. Brent's ego no doubt fed that emotion but I intended to replace it with a better one now.

"Fuck yeah I ohhh man," he gasped as I tickled that soft spot behind his sack where it met his butt crack. "Ohhh...sssoo... offff... aaaa...aahhh!" Brent pushed his waist up higher to allow easier access. His pole was so hard it could have pounded nails. Its head was full, red, and, ready to pop. I avoided touching it. He would blow but only at the critical time. I worked his juice sack further.

"This is the feeling you always get from swimming too," I said firmly.

"Feeling...swimming...same...ohhh helllll," he nodded quickly.

"You get turned on big time by swimming," I stated as I gently began to run my other free palm under his dick. The veins there throbbed with urgency. Brent's blaster was at full staff and soon my palm felt slick with his precum.

"Turned ooo...yyeesss...I...I...I... dooooowww," Brent agreed urgently. His need to explode was growing and with it, a new connection between swimming and sexual release was being made thanks to the tape he was seeing and the stimulations his mind was getting.

"When you see the pool at the swim meet you will remember how aroused you are right now." I commanded as I quickened my ball and cock work on my zonked jock.

"See pool...totally aroused...yesss...oohh yessssss," he moaned as his body moved his waist up and down causing his engorged pole to rub faster across my open palm.

."Your body will react just like now. Got it?" I growled fiercely.

"My body...my body...yessss...oh god fucking yesssss," he howled as his cock's head cried out to erupt.

"See the pool water at the meet," I urged to my prey while I softly enclosed my hand around his meat. "Feel the warm water's pressure on you body. On your cock, your balls," I cooed as I enfolded Brent's nuts with my other hand and began to lightly squeeze.

"The water... shit... hot...turned on...the fucking water...on my balls oh...damnnnn," Brent babbled.

"Even when you are in the water...you feel it stroking your body, your balls, and your cock. It hits your ass too and you love it there even more." I increased my pump on his dick and squeezed his balls tighter. "When its warmth fills your crack you got to pop!"

"Stroking...stroking my bod...oh so hot...my cock...my nuts...my ass... fuck...got...to...to pop...oh fuck... yeahhhhh," Brent growled lost in a sexual need to cum.

"Say it again," I asked as I hit stride to bring my jock-boy to climax!

"MY ASS... FEELING... WARM... IN MY ASS...OH...MY BALSSS...SHIT...I'M...OHHH FUCCC." Brent screamed in sexual frenzy. I pulled on his nuts one last time and stroked my varsity swimmer over the line. My hunky pup blew his cork. His hot jis flew into the air as I continued pumping his well. He collapsed in the chair. His mouth opens as he gasped for air. Brent's 'mental prep' had taken place. It was not the one he had planned but it would do. I left him there after placing a keyword in his brain. When I said it, my swimming star would return to a pliable hypnotic state suitable for further programming.

A Boner Book

Part Three:
Swimmer's Meat at the Meet

It was the weekend of the big meet. Sean and I took our seats in the stands and prepared for the show. The teams began their races while we both waited anxiously for Brent's big event. Finally, it was time. Brent, along with Enrico took their slots at the pool's edge along with opponents from the opposing sides. This race would decide which school won the meet.

"Brent is the favorite but Enrico is better," Sean whispered to me, "he just needs to get a victory under his belt and get Brent's razzing off his back. Great definition too huh?"

I turned to Sean smiling, "should I be jealous big bro," I teased.

"No way," laughed Sean, "you own this butt." My macho bottom-boy then slapped one of his muscular cheeks. He turned back to the meet while I gave my stud-boy a quick once over. Prime, yes sir. "Jesus, look over there." He cried softly and nodded toward the swimmers. There was the school's team favorite standing on the pool's edge with his eyes locked on the water and...yes, sporting one fucking huge hard-on in his Speedos. I mean the dude's front was tent-poled!

The other swimmers had their focus on Brent who just stood there gazing at the pool. The crowd hooted in derision at the sight. They got even more boisterous when Brent's right hand disappeared down the front of his waistband and started masturbating himself under his suit!

"Fucking soooo turned on," my zapped swimmer moaned out loud in a tone that echoed throughout the gym. Oh, this is the bomb. The crowd roared with the loudest yell from Brent's horrified brother who, along with his firemen buddies, had come to see big Craig's little jock brother perform. Well, he was I guess at that.

"What the fuck are you doing man?" Screamed an enraged and embarrassed Craig. I took in the fire-stud big brother. About 36, 6', 220lbs of beefy muscle with a black buzz cut, some dark hair curling up from his open collar and, from the look of it when he rose up in his seat in those tight fire pants, a tasty meaty butt and front basket as well. This was the 'faggot' abuser. Another check off in my brain. I returned my gaze to the pool.

"Fucking warm on me," Brent blissfully gurgled as he continued his cock stroking moves, "Up my ass...fucking hot." With that comment big brother's face went scarlet. He shut up and slowly sat down in his seat. His colleagues on the force tried not to look at him or Brent. It soon got worse for big brother Craig.

"Yeah, so fucking hot up my ass," gasped Brent in a roar as he threw his head back, "here it comes!" The gym echoed with Brent's cry of "FUUUCCCKKK... HOTTT... UPPP...MYYYY...ASSSS... YYEEAAHHHH". The crowd sat stunned in silence. Craig's firemen buddies quietly got up and left leaving the macho fireman in the center of an empty circle of seats. When he realized that quite a few eyes from the crowd had now trained their eyes on him, he beat a fast path out of the stands.

It was fantastic. There was dead silence in the gym and time froze. A concerned Enrico left his place at the pool edge, moved to Brent and, shook him. Brent snapped out of it. He shot a puzzled glance at the young Latino teammate and was probably going to shove him away until he realized his right hand was otherwise occupied. Brent's panicked gaze circled around the gym till it hit Craig's scowling face by the exit door. Brent removed his hand from his rapidly deflating manhood. He was humiliated in front of his big brother. Craig shook his head and turned to leave.

Everyone quickly retook their positions but this time Brent was focused not on the pool but, intently on Craig's disappearing form. In fact, he so concentrated on his older brother's disapproving visage that he missed the start off signal and left the blocks a few seconds late. Unfortunately Enrico, who had glanced over at Brent to make sure his teammate was still ok, also came late off the blocks. The crowd roared as the swimmers raced the distance. In the end thanks to an amazing display of strength and desire, our side had won. Thanks, that is to Enrico who came up fast to make up time lost and burn up the competition. Later we watched as his time was posted. Enrico had not only shattered Brent's school time but also the entire nations. As he whopped it up with his teammates, a glowering Brent stood in the loser's circle. The team had a new star!

The next day the school was a blaze with two topics of discussion. Enrico's amazing victory and whether or not Brent had really cum in his Speedos in the gym. Many were also secretly snickering about how Brent had done 'whatever' while moaning about something warm going up his ass!

Part Four:
While We're Out Together Dancing Cheek To Cheek

Things got intense at school after that. Naturally Brent got suspended from the team since ever time he got near the pool water he zoned out and started...well you know. Enrico came into his own as a star school swimmer and out as a gay one to boot. Always liked that guy. We became buds fast and he confided in me that his home life was hell due to an older brother who served on the local police force. A regular hunk built stallion among the ladies who trained at the gym I worked at. Seems he gave his 'pussy' younger brother a hell of a lot of crap for not 'scoring on chicks like a real man' as he put it. Another check went off in my brain.

Brent however was unfinished business. I had planted a key word in him that would send him back into a hypnotic state. The when and where of finishing him off was my problem. But as fate would have it, the mountain came to me when Sean left for an away weekend wrestling tournament a few weeks after that infamous swim 'meat/ meet'. My parents had gone with him to cheer him on while I was stuck doing a school project at home all weekend by myself. It was a bummer missing my bottom-boy do his stuff but this was a project that had to be done. Turns out that weekend I got two projects completed. I had just finished the school one when someone came to the door. Yep, it was Brent!

"Brent," I said somewhat in shock, "what are you doing here?" He just glared at me and pushed his way in.

"Listen you pansy assed fagot." He angrily said as he grabbed my shirt with one hand and put a fist near my face. "I'm popping boners every time I'm near water and, there is a rumor you got something to do with it. I think the rumors are right! I'm going to fuck you up bad." He drew in close for the kill. I knew I had to move fast.

"TOP DOG"! I uttered swiftly. Brent's eyes glazed and his body went slack. The keyword I'd programmed into him weeks ago came to life! I walked around my hypnotic captive and smiled. "I think, you arrogant fucker, that you are the one getting 'fucked up'. Gently I ran the side of my hand across the handsome face of the zonked athlete. An idea hit me.

"Strip you bastard and ah...do it slow and sexy." I commanded.

Brent began to sway his hips in time to some imaginary music letting me take in the erotic scene of a hot straight jock doing a highly charged striptease. Silently he unbuttoned his shirt, exposed his hard leanly muscled but defined swimmer's body, and let the shirt drop to the floor.

"Play with your tits boy," I ordered. My zapped hunk complied moving his hands up to his soft brown pubs. He rubbed each one gently making sure to squeeze and tweak them. "Shittt," he whispered as the brown orbs hardened. Brent increased his massage on them till they stood up rock hard and bullet pointy. I noticed that his crotch basket was showing signs of arousal as well. The hypnotized stud continued his tit play with one hand as the other moved down his chest, past his six-pack, and cupped his basket. His hips still swayed and he turned erotically giving me a nice view of his cute butt hidden in those jeans.

"Drop those pants cunt-boy," I said.

Brent unbuckled his pants and slid them off. He stopped for a few seconds to get them past his thighs then, continued his sexual gyrations. Those muscular legs reflected his pool - workouts. His tight white cotton underwear fit snuggly in front and back. I walked over to my swaying hunk and glided my hands across his warm tender inner thighs then; I inserted them up his legs bands to enfold his balls in my grip. He was hot, moist; the flesh was soft to my touch. I removed my hands and had Brent drop the final shield to his soon to be toppled 'instrument of straightness'. His firm, marble-white, dimpled butt was so fuckable. His meat, now semi hard, was framed by that set of nuts that now swung in rhythmic time to his hip movements.

"Finger that butt hole pussy while you play with your sack," I insisted. Brent bent slightly at the knees and reached down with one hand and rolled his balls while the other sensually slide down his crack and into its deep crevice. "How does that feel jock?" I smirked as Brent finger fucked himself before my eyes. His dick rose to full staff. "Ohhh... fffuucccc." Brent rasped hoarsely. He was ready!

"Brent," I said firmly. "Remember how you feel when you see water?"

"Yessss," he sighed as he continued his anal and testicular maneuvers on himself. "It feels hot,"

"It's hot and powerful right?" I went on. Brent nodded. He was in sexual heat to judge by a fully erect dick, which had precum hanging down from its slit and hitting the floor in one long strand of translucent white.

"Hot. Powerful," Brent acknowledged.

It totally arouses you." I went on.

"Yes, hot powerful...total high," my stimulated dancer, agreed.

"Man sex is like water," I suggested smiling.

"Man sex...likes water." Brent repeated. His brain centers were at maximum capacity for manipulation and it was time to go for it.

"Sex with men is warm and powerful. Wet, warm and, powerful just like water." I instructed. "Repeat it."

"Sex with men is wet, warm, and powerful." He replied.

I reached down to stroke his cock. "Feel the warmth, the power. It's beyond sex with women." I chanted slowly as I fed his control panel its new marching orders.

Brent's cock throbbed in my hand. "Men sex...better...fucking hotter," he whispered.

"Women don't arouse you anymore." I insisted as I went for the final piece.

"No arousal women. Men...sex...with...ohh damm I'm hot." My dazed jock muttered as I took over his ball job too. He continued his ass screwing with his fee hand returned to minister to his nipples. Brent's breathing intensified. His brain was rapidly processing the information he was receiving and the sexual overload I was giving it.

"Need man-sex. You need man-sex." I hurriedly replied. "You ass likes cock in it!"

"I need man sex." He nodded as his mouth slackened. "My ass needs cock in it." He increased the tempo of his finger insertions. Judging his hip thrusts of his rod through my hands while he was doing it and the flickering of his eyelids he was close to breaking apart. Time to clinch the deal.

"You need cock. You want warm cock juices in you. You love to eat cum. You hate sex with woman. Women turn you sexually off." I yelled into his face abruptly. "You want to be the woman with a guy. You love being a pussy!"

"I NEED COCK. I NEED COCK. WOMEN DON'T TURN ME ON. A PUSSY. I AM A PUSSY." He shouted as his eyes stop flickering and his hip thrusts quickened. I had done it. I had rewired his mind turning a cunt crazy jock into a cock crazy one.

"Men turn you on so bad you can cream right now!" My voice echoed in his mind.

"MEN...OOH SHIT...MEN...TURNED ON BYY THEMMM... GGGGOT TO BLOOOOWWWW...OOOOOHHHH." He screamed.

"Blow your wad then you bastard," I hooted. "Spill out that hot man juice. Remember, when you cum now you will be admitting that you are a cum crazed boy-cunt from now on." I squeezed his balls and pushed his cock to point up to his arrogant face. As I did, he exploded sending his cum past his chin to hit his upper lips and nose.

Brent's slipped to his knees exhausted by the powerful sexual high I had him on. He gazed dully ahead and repeatedly sighed in a dull chant that was music to my ears "Love cock. Love cock. Need men. Need cum. Ass fuck, need it bad."

I stared at him. On his knees, telling the world of his new sexual desires all while licking the cum off his face with his tongue. "Fucking hot." He muttered as he ingested his cum and with it forever sealing the loss of his straightness. "Man juices are sooooo hot." He giggled girlishly.

"What the fuck is this," a voice from the doorway stated. I turned to see a smiling Enrico nodding in glee at the sight of Brent down there on his knees with cum on his face and fingering his butt hole. "Ghees, Eric told me the dude was on his way here so we kicked butt to get here in case you needed help," he chuckled. "But fuck man you cleaned stud boy's clock but good. Right Eric?"

It was then I noticed a stunned Eric behind Enrico.

"Eric," I stammered, "it's not what you think."

"I think you turned Brent into a pussy," said Eric sternly. The air grew quiet until suddenly Eric broke out laughing. "And that is sooo cool," my blonde buff swimmer said in glee.

"You...ahh," I was confused and it showed.

"It is cool man," Enrico assured me. "Since Brent was kicked off the team old Eric and I found we had a lot in common and I mean A LOT!" The young Latino reached over and put his arm over the blonde stud, kissed him on the cheek, and winked at me. "Eric's my lover bro. I was going to tell you but wanted Eric to get comfortable in it."

"Yeah," said a blushing Eric, "I kinda knew for awhile but Brent put the fear of God in me about coming out so I..." his voice trailed off. "Then being around Enrico..."

We all looked at Brent who was still on his knees licking up the cum from his face and fingering his chute. The bastard had done a lot of damage and we all knew that it was time for payback in a big way.

"Hey guys," I laughed. "How about we make a movie." The two jocks looked at me in a puzzled way. "And I got just the star for it!" I stated.

Part Five:
Top Dog

"Are you sure I won't be recognized?" Eric asked as he adjusted the black leather mask on his head. He was dressed in a pair of black leather chaps with matching front-laced black leather jockstrap. Across his well-defined pecs, there were two crossed bands. His hard lean swimmers build filled out nicely in leather bindings and the outfit only emphasized his sexual allure.

"Man I don't even recognize you. You look fucking amazing," said Enrico as he glanced over from behind the video camera. The hunky Latino grinned at his transformed teammate with ill-disguised lust and a telltale bulge in his jeans. Eric broke out into a smile and his black cod piece protruded out a bit more; it was obvious to me that these two were seeing each other in a new way for the first time.

"Well guys I hate to break this up," I interrupted as both jocks refocused on me. "But to quote some old MGM flick: Let's put on a show!"

Enrico got busy at the camera, Eric did a quick set of pushups, and situps to not only pump up the goods but also to give his hot leather-covered body a nice sheen of sweat. I brought in our major performer." Gentlemen," I hoped mockingly, "I give you the star of our video: Pussy Puppy!"

With that, I lead in Brent who came in on all fours suitably attired in a black leather studded dog collar and a flimsy leather thong. He looked great with his basket straining in a crotch-costume that was two sizes too small for the items that were to be covered. The tip of his cock was just barely visible at the top of the black waistband while his balls protruded slightly out on each side to give the entire piece a forward sexy thrust. His hard dimpled muscular jock-butt shone like white marble under the lights we had set up. I stepped out of camera range and signaled Eric to begin.

Eric walked up to his puppy and said gruffly, "Brent say hello doggy style."

Brent lifted his head, "arf...arf," he barked as he wagged his exposed butt to the camera. His swimmer toned body rippled with each sway.

"Come here straight boy," Eric commanded. Brent crawled up close until his nose was in direct contact with Eric's package. "Sniff what a real man smells like," our leather master snarled in contempt. Brent pushed his nose deep in and the camera recorded our macho boy's expanding chest as he sucked in the funky sexy scent of hot crotch wrapped in leather.

Eric pushed Brent back and stared at his pup. "You want a taste?" He asked. "Does pussy puppy want to slobber on his master's bone?"

Enrico zoomed in to capture the delirious look of hunger on Brent's face. His sensual features were a vision of pure animal lust and I could see his meat pushing hard on the flimsy thong. I signaled Enrico to get it in the shot but the hunky Latino was already on it. Brent moaned in desire and his tongue licked his lips. The straight dude was turning out to be one lusty cock-hound!

"Beg boy," stated Eric. "Show me how a good pussy pup begs."

Brent rapidly rose up on his haunches holding his arms up at either side and keeping his tongue hanging out. Eric reached over pulled Brent's head very close to his crotch. Brent's tongue flicked out and licked at the lacings. "Need..." he gasped, "Need it so bad sirrrr."

"What dog," asked a smug leather master to his prey? "Tell me what a young straight jock stud always needs."

"I need to suck that bone master," Brent babbled. "I need man cock sir. I FUCKING NEED MAN-COCK." He yelled.

"Lick my crotch you pussy pup," he growled sexily as he permitted jock hunk Brent's tongue to run up and down Eric's jockstrap. Brent, the babe seducer master went wild. Can there ever be anything hotter than watching a straight jock down on all fours, dog collared, sporting a hard-on in leather thong, tongue out slobbering to give a leather master 's basket a hot moist bathe and, filling the air around him with cries indicating his sheer devotion to man-cock. Okay there are two more scenes that rank up there but hell, give the movie time dudes! Eric relaxed and enjoyed the oral service of his former hero. Judging by his bulging meat in that codpiece good old, Brent gave good service. Eric reached down to pat his pouch's head. Enrico signaled me he had got it all on tape. "Go on boy," Eric encouraged. "Get inside my leather."

Brent reached up to unlace his master's bone but had his hand slapped away quickly by Eric.

"Use your teeth cunt," snarled Eric.

Brent uttered a gut-wrenching moan of pure surrender and proceeded to unlace Eric's raging manhood with his teeth. As the laces came undone, the young leather master's pole sprung out and slapped Brent across the face. Priceless dude. Priceless.

"Want this," Eric laughed sharply as he slapped his pecker across Brent cheeks. Brent's eyes looked ravenous as spittle dripped from his open mouth. Oh yeah, he wanted it. That former cunt man was now thoroughly cock happy. "Then suck it you bastard." Eric whispered heatedly as he guided his monster meat into Brent's waiting mouth.

"UUUMMMPPHH," a cock filled mouth of Brent tried to reply. The school's star athlete greedily slurped away as he got his dog owner's manhood all nice and slick for future uses. Brent's cock-head was sticking further out of his thong and the material by the slit was wet and gooey.

"Good puppy" Eric laughed after a few minutes of Brent's oral chow downing. He reached further down to rub Brent pac. The effect was priceless as Brent flopped onto his back and howled in pleasure at his belly rub. His arms and legs flayed about while his cock rose up further out of a waistband showing signs of a wider wet patch.

"Tell me." Stated Eric, "Tell me like a dog how much you like the touch of a man on your belly?"

The room filled with Brent's quick cries, "WOOF. WOOOF. WOOOF."

Eric reached down further, spread apart Brent's hard thighs, and ran his finger over Brent's crack. Brent's head began to move back and forth in excitement as Eric slipped his hand between the swimmer's cheeks to massage that inner tender skin. "Okay boy, tell me what you want now, and speak normally." Eric said while his hand rubbed further into his pooch's crack. We had all agreed that to really work the audience would need more from Brent that animal noises and I had so instructed Eric.

"I want my ass full sirrrr," groaned Eric who was obviously in heat. "Puppy needs cock sirrrr."

"Are you sure bitch?" Eric rasped as he, in full camera view, lifted up one of Brent's legs so Enrico could zero in as Eric inserted his finger into Brent's hole. The camera recorded the jock's outer ring yielding to the invader. Watching that soft moist muscular chute-ring contract and relax, as Eric's finger-fucked away in it was hot let me tell you!

"OHHH... FFUUCCC," Brent howled as the finger in him hit home. "My cunt needs to get fuckkkkkked." Brent kept up a steady stream of begging whimpers while Eric continued the initial scew job on the once haughty jock. Brent would never live down the words he said then:

"Fuck me sir."

"Slip it in my pussy hole."

"Take my ass like the bitch I am sir."

It was amazing watching Brent grovel to get finger fucked. One week ago, he was a cocky arrogant straight jock bastard. Today he was a pitiful cock crazed cunt dying to fill his openings by a guy. Damn it was sweet.

"FUCK Meee," he pleaded. "Oh dam my chute needs you sir."

Eric then flipped him over and slapped Brent's marble white ass. "Up on all fours you bitch!" he commanded. As Brent, complied Eric landed a series of slaps on that jock butt.

SLAP

"OOHH YEESS," cried Brent.

SLAP. SLAP. SLAP. SLAP. Came the sounds as Eric butt slapped the jock - hunk.

"Fucking turn my ass red sir," Brent begged. Yep when a straight jock goes for cock, he loses it bad. After a few more whacks and that marble white butt was fire engine red. Considering Brent's brother career, I wondered if he might be needed right now to help dose his little stud brother's sexual fires. Hmmm...ah later.

Eric stopped then walked around to face his dog-boy. He undid his codpiece's laces fully and exposed his stiff meat to a dazed and ravenous looking Brent. "I want it slicker punk. You want my bone some more boy?" He rasped gruffly as Brent's head nodded furiously in agreement. The former straight athlete's tongue hung out dripping with desire.

"May I suck your bone sir?" He whimpered submissively, "This pansy assed dog needs it so bad sir."

Eric guffawed and inserted his cock into that mouth that had once ridiculed gays and spouted its own vaunted straight masculinity. The camera captured good old Brent, good old heterosexual and haughty Brent, slobbering away on leather-man's cock like he was a cheap whore!

"Oomph, more, more." He slurped as he deep throated Eric pole.

At one point, he then broke off to lick his leather master's balls. Eric pulled away, turned his butt to Brent's face. Spreading his powerfully developed cheeks Eric wiggled his exposed asshole at the delirious puppy. "Want to eat my ass boy." He rasped.

"Fuck yes, sir!" hooted Brent as he dove into those bubble cheeks. The room filled with Eric's breathing and the unmistakable sounds of a hungry dog's munching.

"UUUMMPPHH," Brent muttered as his muffled voice came from its hiding place deep in Eric crack. Eric's dick was ready to blow from the rimming he was getting. I signaled him that it was time for the 'money shot'.

He pulled away from his pup to reveal Brent's sexually blissful face covered in saliva. Eric quickly went to Brent's rear, spread jock boy's cheeks, and, asked the killer question. "What do you want bitch?"

"I want you to fuck my ass sir," begged Brent as he wiggled his butt aggressively. "I'm so fucking hot for it sir. My puppy-pussy is wet for it."

Eric nodded to the camera and drove his rod home. "TAKE IT YOU BITCH!" he roared as his dick burst into virgin fields.

"Aaahhhh...yyeahhh...getting fucked," a slacked jawed Brent, cried as the camera recorded the deflowering and how Brent's eyes rolled back in his sockets in a sublime joy. Our 'star' moaned in pleasure with each thrust (well score one for big brother Craig, huh, but he should have said it was really straight hunky jocks that moan as they get plowed). "Fuck my hole. Yeah get it deeper sir." Brent encouraged as he began to piston his hips back and forth to help in his screwing.

Enrico, who by now had dropped his pants and was stroking his own impressive hard-on signaled to me to take the camera. When I did, he walked up to Brent's face and pushed his honey-toned Latin meat right up to the 'star' mouth. Brent instantly opened up to savor the treat. "Take my dick you arrogant asshole," Enrico growled. Soon the three of them were at it hot and heavy (I made sure Enrico's face was out of every shot).

Eric reached down to stroke Brent's engorged cock and it was obvious that a climax for all three was imminent. Sure enough, I soon heard the cry.

"I'M CUMINGGGG," Eric moaned as he thrust deeply between Brent's dimpled butt cheeks and exploded.

Enrico pulled out of Brent's mouth. "TASTE MY SPUNK JOCK-

BOY," he bellowed as he came onto Brents face.

"AAAAHHH FFFUUCCKK," Brent yelled as his own rod burst forth a steady stream of hot cream. It splattered up his chest and dripped from his chin. Brent's dazed, grinning face was covered in both his and Enrico's jis. I filmed his smiling image, tongue out, licking the man-cream around his lips. "Man juices," rasped Brent as he savored each drop.

It was an awesome sight. Brent's deflowering, degradation, and humiliating sexual lusts were now forever recorded for future generations to enjoy. We continued to tape a few more scenes until at last I said the fateful words:

CUT and PRINT! The three of us then cleaned up the set letting Brent do the honors of tongue mopping the floors for any remaining cum.

Later on, I made two copies of our epic. One for public consumption and one 'special' tape for a private audience. Eric, Enrico, and myself watched the public tape later as a docile Brent, still collared and on all fours, hungrily sucked away on our hard cocks. Ever notice how straight young muscle jocks go crazy for cum after their first taste of it? We all had to agree as we saw the finished product: A Star had been borne!

Part Six:
What No Popcorn!

The next day I invited macho fireman Craig over to the house after his shift. He arrived in his fireman's blues. Had to admit that in that tight uniform he was one fucking steamy number. His muscles pressed against the buttons of his shirt. He had undone a few buttons at the top revealing dark curling black chest hair covering an impressive set of pecs. Both his forearms were bulging and I swear he had small melons under each bicep.

"Well what the fuck is this all about?" He snarled as he walked in. "And let me tell you kid I've heard about you and your pansy assed brother so lets get things straight now; touch my ass," he said as he smacked his meaty blue uniformed covered butt, "and I'll bust yours. Got it!"

"Yes sir," I answered with fake fear and submission, "I'd never dream of touching you sexually sir. I know a faggot is never a match for a real man sir." Oh, yeah, right.

Craig smiled smugly. "Good cause my meat," he grabbed his crotch with one of his hands and cradled it so that it pushed up the already tight material to further outline what promised to be one fully rounded sack of potatoes and meat, "is only for bitches."

"Yes sir," I muttered as I fed his macho ego. "I asked you here because... well sir... Brent made this tape sir," I began to sputter so he'd think he had intimidated me. Set him up high then knock out the pins!

"Tape," he replied, "what the fuck are you talking about?"

"It might be better if I showed it to you sir." With that, I pointed to the chair and Brent's big brother sat down to watch the first public showing of 'Dog Bone Production Inc.' (named by courtesy of Eric). A nifty little movie about a pussy pup named Brent! With an underlay of, you need ask.

"Where's the fuckin popcorn?" Craig said sarcastically as he adjusted in the chair. His powerful thighs spread slightly in the seat. Soon they'd spread open farther if things went as planned. I hit play.

The video revved to life and Craig was treated to little brother Brent doing his sexual doggy tricks for a leather-masked man (Eric who at second glance was really into it).

"What the fuck," gasped Craig as he turned to me.

"You better watch it all sir," I said quietly. "It gets worse and he says things about you in parts (a lie but hell he had to focus)."

A pale Craig gazed back at the video. As the movie went on his jaw dropped. The room filled with Brent's voice shouting (or moaning you decide) such choice lines as:

"Fuck my straight pussy sir! I need it soooo bad!""

"AAAHHHWWWHHHOO...AARRFF AARRFF!"

And my own personal favorite: "Please feed me that bone sir!"

Craig was mesmerized. I guess at first, cause he was watching his athletic little brother being thoroughly degraded and loving every minute of it but later, cause the programming in the tape had locked onto his brain.

I let the movie run its course. Hey, you don't stop art! When it ended, I flicked off the machine and turned to Craig. He was staring blank eyed.

"COME HERE!" I ordered. My hunky fireman got up and walked to me. I pulled his shirt roughly open, popping his remaining buttons and, releasing that massive chest into full view.

"Big brother you work out," I chuckled as I undid his belt and dropped his pants. I reached for the waistband of his tight white cottons and slowly exposed his more intimate charms. Hung like the proverbial horse with balls to match. An uncut mouth watering treat if you didn't count his meaty butt. Relax, I did count it, hehehe!

I jiggled his balls in my palm. "I'm afraid I lied Mr. Fireman when I said I wouldn't touch you sexually. Am I forgiven, hmmm?" I chuckled. "In fact this is only the start." I bent over and kissed his full sensual lips. Hmmm tasty too!

"Okay boys, are we ready to permanently hose down the fires of this muscle built fucker's sexual image," I said as a smiling Enrico and Eric entered the room. Each was ready for the action. Hell, Eric even brought 'Dog Bones' biggest (and so far only) star performer with him. Good old reformulated pussy boy Brent who bounded in on all fours suitably collared and leashed. Dogboy Brent raced up and sniffed at his zonked brother's crotch. Watching him, bark at Craig was too cool. When Brent stuck his nose up Craig's butt crack to further sniff, we all lost it. After that, we went to work on Craig. But, that's a whole nother tale gents!

My Brother's Keeper IV: Fire In The Hole!

Part One:
When We Last Left Our Hero

"OOHHHH fucccc..." Craig groaned as his little brother Brent continued eating his humpy older brother 's beefy muscular butt out for the camera. We had decided to do a quick production for 'Dog Bones Inc.' while we reprogrammed our fireman hunk. A bit of editing would be required to delete 'our roles' in the fun but hey no problem. After all, we all must sacrifice for art, right?

Enrico and Eric had positioned the self-proclaimed fag hater Craig belly down and butt up on a desk and then let our 'star' Brent have at him. Eric was zooming in making sure that the camera was getting a nice view of that chute getting its first man on man rimming. Old Craig was a natural in front of the camera. His hot six-foot 220lb solid muscular frame was gyrating on the desktop in a bump and grind that got us all hard. Every once in awhile he'd rise up a bit to give a nice shot of his hefty balls and stiff, uncut thick hose.

"Hmmm," growled our 'star' as his tongue bathed his brother's cherry hole making sure that the black curly hairs in there were glistening with saliva. Craig's ring was contracting in a series of spasms to its bathe. Looking at it just winking at the viewer was almost too much. But there was time enough for that. Old firefighter Craig was about to have an experience in the fires within!

I walked up to face our stud making sure to signal Eric to keep focus on the action in the rear so to speak. I bent down close to whisper in our zapped hunk's ear. "Feeling good there, bro?"

"Ooohhh mannn...feeling great," he gasped lost in sexual heat and mentally off balanced by the hypnotic trance we had put him under. Poor old (if 36 is old...looking at this muscled beefy hunk, trust me it ain't) Craig was too distracted offer any resistance. Hell, straight or gay when a guy is being guided by the organ between his legs the one between his ears is easy prey to anything and the 'anything' on today's blue plate special was me! Craig's powerful thighs spread further apart as his younger brother burrowed in deeper with his tongue. Craig's breathing intensified. He was primed. Okay fire boy get ready to experience a mental meltdown.

"Go with it Craig. Fell the hot moist heat down there." I teased wickedly. "Hot right?"

"Yeah, so fucking hot," Craig, agreed as his hips began to hump the desk. Watching that hefty hot body move up and down was some sight. This boy was one powerfully built piece of meat. With that black buzz cut hair and lightly furred chest Brent's big bro was a man's dream fuck. Turning this fag-hater into a fag lover would be a gift to men.

"You love it man," I repeated, "it's so hot... it's making you so hard!"

"Bet you assss... aarrghh," he roared as Brent increased his mouth actions. Craig was sweating bullets and grinding on the desktop. I hoped the wood held up under him.

"You will always remember every second of this." I said in a firm quiet voice. "Your mind will relive each hot second of how you feel right now and your body will relive everything its feeling right?" I stated.

"Oh... yeah... in mind... in body." Craig nodded furiously. I indicated to Enrico to give Brent a prearranged signal. Enrico caught Brent eye and stuck a finger in his own mouth Brent lit up and did the same. Then inserted it in and out in Craig's chute while still licking his big brothers hole. Craig howled as his chute got its first prostate massage. The zonked fire stud began to seriously screw the desktop. He was close.

"You will remember how hot this was. You will relive it all." I ordered as a sexually delirious Craig rapidly nodded. He was too hot to fight anything I ordered. "You will think of this whenever I talk about fire equipment." I instructed. "No matter where or when it will flood your mind and you will not be able to resist getting turned on. You will also slip back into this hypnotic trance and do whatever I suggest."

"Yes...yes... hot... fire talk...you suggest... return to trance... oh fuck... I can't hold it innnnnn," he moaned as he hit the 'wall' so to speak. Our zonked side of beef let out a roar, slammed his powerful butt into the desk, and then collapsed panting in exhaustion. The final film shot was focused on the cum that was oozing out from under his powerful hips. Dog Bone's Inc. had another future star!

Part Two:
Fireside Chats

Craig and I walked into the station's living quarters. As we did, the firemen looked up. "Now this is where my fellow fire fighting brothers live while on duty," Craig explained. I had 'suggested' to Craig that he take me on a tour and, of course, he readily agreed. "You can learn a lot here." He boasted. True I thought as I gazed over the men. Most were average looking but two were prime studs. I was introduced to everyone and took particular time meeting those two.

One was a stunning black man named Tex (guess why). He was about 35, six foot, and built like God had paid attention. He had a dazzling smile and sultry brown eyes. His fire uniform clung tight, emphasized his bulging muscles, and rounded basket. The other hunk was named Mark. I found out later that he was 34. A real Italian cutie that was sporting an impressive physique himself. Yeah both hot and from prior information I secured from Craig both suspected by him of being, in his words, real faggots.

I sat down as Craig strutted to his chair. I had decided to block his memories of encounters with me prior to this in order to have some fun with the fag bashing old Craig. "I am so grateful guys that Craig let me come here." I gushed. "I really want to be a fireman like Craig." I continued.

"Yeah kid just like me." Craig grinned smugly.

"Yeah," I agreed. "I mean grabbing a long hose, right Craig," I smiled as my words hit his brain.

Craig's face grimaced slightly. "Yeah grabbing a hose," he muttered as he shifted in his seat.

"I mean those long thick hoses must be hard to grab." I rattled on innocently as Craig squirmed in his chair.

"Thick hoses...getting grabbed," he sighed as he started to grind into his chair and slip into a trance. The other firemen looked over at him. I could see the puzzled looks they were giving each other.

"I mean," I repeated eagerly, "Watching some guy pull out that long heavy thick hose and pushing on the nozzle."

"God dam heavy hose getting grabbed and pulled," Craig moaned as he continued grinding his meaty muscle butt into the seat cushions while one of his hands started rubbing his thickening cock. The other guys were in shock. Well all but two who, judging from their grins, were enjoying the sight of muscle boy getting turned on.

"Getting the fit on the hydrant nice and snug," I babbled on merrily, "feeling that tight screw lock on nice and tight."

"Getting the screw on... tight... yeah so fucking tight," Craig moaned as he stroked his stiff cock under his pants and began to slip his other free hand down under his ass.

Brent's fag bashing brother was masturbating in front of his 'brothers' and from the look of them he'd never live it down.

"Then feeling the water rush through the thick hose." I chuckled.

"Yeah spurting out from deep inside," replied Tex as he turned to wink at me and nod at Mark.

"Spurting out," Mark seconded.

"Water from deep in the pipe bursting out," I agreed. Craig was at the edge now. He was rubbing his ass and crotch now and moaning in deep guttural tones. "Fucking coming out, yeah."

"I mean the power of the thrusting water must be intense?" I suggested.

"Oh that powerful thrust," growled Craig as he rubbed his butt and quicken his stroke on his rod.

"Then feeling that last ram through," I added. "It must blow out so hot?"

"The last ram," Craig gasped as he gripped his outlined cock and squeezed.

"Yeah," I can see it cumin now!" I laughed as I drove macho boy over the cliff. "Bursting out now right."

Craig threw back his head and grabbed his rock hard cock's outline. "Fucking got to burst nowwwwaaaooowwww." He yelled as he erupted. His pants showed a growing stain. The room was silent. Then reality of it hit the squad

"ARE YOU FUCKING CRAZY?" Yelled the captain as he snapped back from the shock of what had happened.

"Huh," a dazed Craig said as he shook his head, felt dampness in his crotch, and then looked down in horror at what he must have done. He had cum in his uniform pants and in front of the whole squad. "I... I," he tried to speak.

"You are a disgrace to that uniform. And to pull this in front of an innocent kid." The captain continued as he turned to me. I looked appropriately shocked and embarrassed.

"But... but," Craig stuttered.

"In my office now," the captain barked.

"Captain," asked Tex. "The kid looks really shook up. Mark and I will take him home if it's ok?"

The captain glanced at me. I feigned mock horror. Hey, such talk and me a minor too. The captain quickly agreed. I walked out with the two humpy firemen.

"Okay kid," whispered Tex when we got out of earshot. "I know you did that and all I can say is..." I looked up waiting to see if I was in trouble. "How can Mark and I get in on it?" He smiled.

"Fuck guys," chuckled Mark, "I want to get into Craig!"

We all laughed and walked away from the station while I filled them in and planned Craig's final graduation ceremony from fiery bull to cock hungry heifer.

Chapter Three:
Give It To Me One More Time

I received a call a few days later from Tex. He told me that Craig had been assigned new duty at the old firehouse down in the factory section of town. Since it was a sparsely populated area the station was only had a three-man squad. In an amazing coincidence, Tex and Mark had gotten assigned as the other two. Time to mind fuck old Craig or... fuck whatever.

I arrived at the station to find Craig washing off the truck. He looked as hot as usual with his fireman uniform wet and clinging tightly to his muscular frame. Tex and Mark were watching him as he bent over to clean under the truck. Seeing that bubble butt straining to break out from its pants was erotic as hell. Craig's muscular thighs flexed as he moved. This was going to be one hot bottom boy. As I walked in Craig stood up to face me. He had unbuttoned his shirt in front giving me a great view of his massive manly chest with its light black hairy fur and those quarter-sized nipples. He frowned and growled at me. "What the fuck are you doing here?"

"You look tired Craig," I said slowly.

"Huh," he replied as my words sunk in.

"Yeah," I repeated, "tired very tired. Probably from lifting and grabbing those hoses around."

"Hoses... tired...grabbing," my fire-hunk answered weakly as he sunk back into his trance. He gently swayed as his eyes blinked. My macho fireman was sinking fast.

"It must be so hot to work that hose." I smirked.

"Working that hose... hot," he moaned as his powerful hand moved down to massage his crotch. Tex and Mark just stared silently. They waited for me to do my thing on their firefighting 'brother'. By now, Craig was really swaying and I could see his man-meat's rigid outline in his pants.

"Feels so good," I said firmly, "You are so turned on when you listen to me right."

"Oh shit yesss," he hissed as he rubbed his rod. He stroked himself faster and began to press his massive thighs together squeezing his sack as he squirmed.

"Strip boy," I said sharply. Time to rewire Craig to serve his two 'brothers better!

Craig pulled off his shirt revealing that massive hard toned body. Then he bent and dropped his pants. He stood there buck naked with his impressive 9" uncut thick meat already at ½ mast. He was now pumping it to full steam.

"Work that meat boy," I growled. "And play with those tits of yours, boy."

Craig sighed as he played with his cock. His other hand started to caress his chest running through his hairy pecs and playing with each nipple. He started to move as he turned on and his ball sack gently began to sway. That boy had a nice set of hefty low hangers. I turned to the other guys. They were stripping fast.

"Feeling hot punk boy?" I rasped as I felt the sexual heat rising in the room.

"Fuck yeah," growled Craig as he turned up his stimulations. Tex walked over to Craig. His muscled dark toned body was a searing contrast to Craig's pale skin. Tex's meat was a stiff 10" of man meat and as he stepped behind Craig, I knew where it was going to wind up. He reached around Craig with one of his arms and took over massaging Craig's chest. My zonked straight boy leaned back and gave a muted cry. He was flying.

"Tex and Mark are your brother firefighter's, right boy?" I said making sure to continually use the term 'boy' to drive home a new self-image.

"Fuck yeah," gasped Craig as Tex played with his 'boy's' chest. Mark walked over (yep, I had guessed right. He had a compact an olive skinned muscle body) Mark placed Craig's hand on his 9" boner. Craig massaged Mark's rod like a natural. The scene was amazing. Former fag bashing Craig pumping his meat while giving his one 'brother' a jerk off even as his other 'brother' played with his chest and got him harder.

"You're their boy," I commanded, "You love servicing their needs."

"Fuck I...so hot," Craig babbled as both guys continued their work. Mark bent and began to suck one of Craig's nipples while Tex lowered his hand to play with Craig's balls (Brent had already shown us how hot he and his brother got off on ball play.

"You are their boy. You love to serve them." I repeated.

"Serve...serve...I...boy?" Craig muttered. The room was silent for a moment as the battle in Craig's brain raged. Tex and Mark continued their sexual assault on the zapped studmuffin. He was moaning and his rod was leaking so much you could hear the wet slap of his hand as it pumped his rod. The guys were driving Craig's erotic zones into a fiery inferno.

"You love sex with them...you get off on it bad...it's the best being their punk boy," I insisted.

"Sex...man sex...their pussy," my zonked prey, muttered again. He was losing it. One last touch.

Time to push him over. "WELL!" I yelled.

"FUCK... YES... I...SERVE... MY BROTHER... THEIR BOY!" He screamed. Craig had been sexually engulfed and consumed.

I had won. "You love serving your brothers. It turns you on. You love their bodies. You need their cock in you feeding you. Pleasuring you!" I chanted repeatedly, as Craig's brain soaked it in. His head nodded throughout it all. He was reprogramming for me even as his hormones were raging inside in a daze of sexual frenzy.

"Love my brother's cock," He agreed as his rod rose to full height. "Oh fuck I need their cocks."

Tex and Mark exchanged a grin as Tex put his hands on Craig's shoulders and pushed our 'boy' down on all fours.

"Please feed me." Craig moaned as he reached down to stroke his engorged cock.

Tex laughed. "Hell Mark, our boy's in need."

"My thoughts exactly," he replied as his lifted Craig's chin and ran his cock's head across the waiting lips of the reconstituted formerly straight firefighter. Craig lips parted like the red sea and slurped in his 'brother's' meat. "Oh hell this boy has some mouth," Mark gasped as Craig pistoned on his rod.

"Well I was always more anal myself," chuckled Tex as he spread Craig's cheeks. He looked over to me and I gave him a quick salute.

"Go to it guys." Hey, they had put up with a lot from that cocksucker. Payback big time you bitch, I thought.

Tex gave me the high sign. He spit some saliva on Craig's hole and then put his massive battering ram at the virgin's gate. "Boy get ready to be pussied." He hooted as he pressed home. His dark meat looked hot as it plowed Craig's creamy white ass. Muffled sounds emerged from Craig's mouth but Mark's rod was too firmly implanted in it to clearly hear whatever was coming out. Craig's bull sack swung back and forth like a pendulum with each of Tex's thrust. I watched as each of Tex's drives into his boy's chute rocked Craig forward onto Mark's cock...now THAT was a fucking awesome sight!

Craig finally pulled off Mark's boner. "Oooohhh fucccccc," he roared as he got the opening of his life down there. "Fuck my ass my brother. Fuck me deep sir!"

Mark grabbed Craig's head and guided his mouth back onto his cock. Craig started sucking like a mad man with a huge grin on his face. That boy liked getting fucked!

The three of us spent the rest of that day reinforcing Craig's new sexuality and teaching him all the joyous variations that guys do with other guys in the sack. By the end of our session muscle hunk Craig was a screaming bottom boy who lived to serve his 'brothers'!

Part Four:
The Station House Mascot

A few days later the whole gang gathered at the station for the unveiling so to speak of our new conquest. Craig stood there naked (well does a studded dog collar count)? Nah as Tex lathered his pup up and slowly shaved his boy's crotch bare. Watching as Tex cleaned off Craig's manhood down there was hot. Enrico and Eric were all grins entwined in each other's arms. Mark was busy playing with Brent who was next to him on all fours whimpering happily as he got his belly rubbed by the hunky 34 year old. I was busy leaning back enjoying the warm embrace of my own brother Sean who was too busy behind me nibbling my ear and rubbing his crotch against my butt to care or notice anything. "Later baby." I whispered to him sensually.

"You promise," Sean hissed in a voice that signaled his sexual heat for me. My former straight jock older brother was definitely addicted to cock now... in particular to mine. I nodded and turned slightly to kiss his cheek. Sean licked his lips and pressed up tight against my rump. "Love getting fucked by you sir!" Oh yeah you can count on it bro I mused.

"Good boy," Tex said in that sexy southern drawl as he hefted Craig's meat sack for it's 'cleaning'. "You feeling good."

"Yes sir," snapped Craig who sprouted a huge grin and a nice sized boner as his plumage was shorn away. "A boy needs to be clean sir," he sighed. Tex worked away till Craig's rod and sack were bare. He stood back to admire his work. Tex and Mark had decided to leave the rest of Craig's hair alone a decision that seemed sound as Craig got off on having his chest hair played with and caressed by a pair of strong-callused hands. Shaving Craig's crotch however was a way of symbolically de manning Craig. "A hairy crotch is a sign of a virile man. I am not some hairless punk kid. Guys that shave there are pansy assed bitches!" He once told his fellow firefighters and, in particular, a certain female who slyly suggested the idea to Mark and Tex. Seems Craig had treated her badly when he found out she was gay. He had set out to 'convert her' with the argument, (yeah you guessed) that a real man was what she needed. Failing that, he had made her the butt of some homophobic jokes in the station. Well the worm has turned it seemed a 'real man' was all Craig now needed!

"Nice. Real nice." Tex laughed as an agreeable Craig reached down to fondle his exposed skin. Craig ran his fingers slowly over the sensitized area and began to masturbate with one hand while the other ran across his thigh to reach back, slip between his crack, and finger himself. The sight of that beefy muscular hunk performing for us was mind blowing. Hairy or bare that meat and those potatoes was prime grade A!

"Fucking loves the feel of it," he muttered deeply. "Boy's got to be clean for his men." Yep the worm had truly turned! Tex told me their 'boy' was putting out big time for every gay fireman and cop in the city!

"Oh guys," said Mark who moved his massage to Brent's balls (and you know how THAT affects our boy Brent), "Tex and I had a small alteration done on our new personal mascot, turn around boy," Mark said to our newly shaved 'performer'. Craig continued his hand job while he turned. I looked in amazement then howled in laughter. There in small letters, tattooed on Craig's back just above his crack was the line: 'for best results insert nozzle in here firmly' with a small fire nozzle under it pointing down directly between Craig's cheeks.

I left the station with my brother knowing that I had done my bit for the police and firemen's morale. Enrico and Eric had wandered upstairs to 'test' the bunks. Tex and Mark... well, they had some dogs that needed exercise. As I drove us home, my mind wandered to a conversation I had before we arrived at the station with Enrico. Seems he had an abusive older brother who was a cop and was giving him crap about being a faggot. I had some plans to arrange. But first...

"Gonna put out my fire bro," my Sean groaned as he touched his semi hard boner as I drove the car into the garage of our house.

"Yeah bro," I replied as I unzipped and gently lowered his head into my crotch. "I got just the hose for it!"

MY BROTHER'S KEEPER V: RICKY GOES DOWN FOR THE COUNT

Part One:
Message in the Bottle

Things had been going pretty good so far. The scorecard ran as follows: two arrogant heterosexual high school jocks now recreated into submissive cock hungry sluts and one hunky muscle-bound fireman babe fucker gelded into a docile station house brood mare. Now you might say I should rest on my laurels but remember Enrico was still out there getting total mind shit on his sexuality from his older cop brother. Well, brothers are my specialty and this smug 29-year-old one was too hot a prize not to take down.

At 5'10" of pure defined hard-body with the Enrico's similar honey brown skin tone and sultry brown eyes this older brother, who boxed on the police team, was one true gay wet dream. When he dressed in his tight blue police uniform, which outlined his mouthwatering Latin basket and rounded melon butt it truly was one of the major sites of the neighborhood. Unfortunately, Ricardo (Ricky to everyone) was an egocentric asshole. He was a former golden gloves winner, a star on the police boxing team, and very much aware of his hot body and sultry Latin looks. He also possessed the unique ability to denigrate Enrico's life style to a degree of exquisite proportions. This self proclaimed 'ladies man' let his kid brother know that he felt any guy taking it 'up the ass' was not a man. I eagerly anticipated knocking this boxer's sexuality out cold.

Thanks to Enrico, I knew his brother, Mr. Macho Latino straight cop stud worked out at a private boxing club that happened to be owned by a gay man. After a small bribe (namely free sack time with cock hungry Brent) I arranged with the owner for Ricky to receive a free "complimentary massage" in the club's new private guest room. I got there early and set up the equipment I would need. After all, 'Dog Bone Production, Inc.' couldn't rely on just one sexy star!

I walked out to the main floor and scoped my prey. Ricky was in the center ring sparing with some guy. He was dominating the fight. His hard toned body glistened with a covering sheen of sweat that highlighted his definition. The ridges between his moist hard six-packs were wet and inviting as they flexed with each turn of his waist. He was dressed in electric blue satin trunks that clung damply to his frame and showed off both his tight bubble ass and those sexy well-proportioned thighs. Ricky boxed with catlike grace, moving around the ring in a demonstration of boxing that was steady, fluid, and fucking hot! No doubt, about it, that hunk was fucking grade 'A' prime!

I watched him in action as he danced and weaved around his opponent. He struck his blows precisely and quickly thoroughly in control and knowing it. At one point, he looked out to the crowd and nodded with a self-assured superior grin. Oh yeah baby, I thought, Cold conking that ego will be fun and pressing that hot boxer body into cock slut service will be heaven. Finally, he landed the punch that sent his opponent out cold down onto the mat. He pulled off his helmet. Flashed a killer smile to some women nearby and left the ring. He went up to the women and started talking. I was close enough to hear his smooth lines. The women were mesmerized. Probably due as much to his killer good looks, that deep erotic accented voice, and that sweating hot muscular body he was pressing close to them as to the lines he was using on them. He arranged to meet them later after his 'massage' promising them that he'd be ready to show them some moves they might enjoy even more than what they had just seen. They giggled as he flexed his pecs for them and watched as he turned to go to the guest room. Like them, I stared at his sexy butt. Ricky turned, ran one hand slowly across his wet chest, and winked suggestively; the women smiled and left the room; no doubt, they were all wet in anticipation for what they hoped would be a night that they'd long remember. Too bad, it was not going to happen. I went meet my 'client' and teach him some moves that would rock his world!

I found my latest 'brother' lying on the table I had set up with a towel draped over his butt. He rose up on his elbows and turned his head to face me.

"You the massage guy," he inquired.

"Yes sir," I replied as I gave him the once over. There he was lying there in full glory. His tight defined cop body just ready for... hehehe.

"You any good," he grumbled as he lowered back onto to table and closed his eyes. "My muscles could use a good loosening." He stretched out fully on the table flexing his muscles and obviously showing them off. As I gazed at him, I felt my own cock stirring. Well, all in good time.

"You will be surprised sir," I cheerfully answered as I put on my latex gloves, "just how loose I'll get some of them. After I'm done you'll be a new man." I picked up a bottle of oil that had been laced, courtesy of a doctor friend (well Brent was free that day okay), with a medicinal substance that fell into what has been classed as one of the "psychotropic" drugs. Similar in nature to "truth serum" it shared the characteristics of sodium pentothal in that it induces a mild hypnotic state in the recipient leaving your subject suggestible and pliable. There's nothing about forcing the truth or any BS like that, but it has the properties of leaving the subject mostly without the will to resist. It can be used to make a very resistant subject much more suggestible and vulnerable to hypnosis and also makes it easier to take them much deeper. Kewl, huh?

Like a loving mother with her baby, I gently poured some onto his back. Gently I massaged the drugged oil across his shoulders and tapered back feeling those tight sexy muscles yield to my pressure and enjoying the thought that with every second the oil was seeping through his open pours into his system. He sighed deeply.

"Feels good man," he mumbled as I worked on his shoulder muscles. I moved in long strokes down his muscular back to his buttocks. Even through the gloves, I could feel their hard definition. He was one well-built stud muffin.

"I find that long strokes work best," I whispered as I worked down the small of his back to his ass. "Everything okay there stud?" I teased as I ran my hands down to his buttocks following the defined back muscles to the prize.

"Feeling great guy," Ricky slurred as the drug started to take effect. He would be woozy and soon quite pliable. "Feeling... Rethax... but stop at the towel othay."

"Problem sir?" I innocently asked.

"Don't like thom guy touching my assth," my boxer cop gasped weakly. He was feeling the drugs effects quite nicely.

"You ever have a guy rub you there before," I quizzed.

"Tant... no...puusth." Ricky answered slowly. "Fucth that feels gooth" he hissed as I stroked his muscles downward from the shoulders to the towel. He stretched out further treating me to a series of muscular movements of his cut and defined body. "Justh leave off my asss."

No pussy huh, I thought as I worked over my boxer's form. Soon my Latin heartthrob. "Just relax and enjoy the long strokes there baby. Remember it's all in the long strokes." I chuckled as I ran my palms across his body savoring the exploration. His cut boxer build was erotic as hell and knowing that he was also homophobic, a jock, and a cop was icing on the cake.

"Long throkes..." my drifting stud boy replied as he drifted off. I slipped one hand under the towel and found my macho boy had no reaction. Feeling that he was ready, I pulled back his towel and exposed his beautiful hard ass to full view. Ricky didn't budge. He just lay there with a blissful look on his handsome face. He was zapped. I ran my hands across his honey toned glorious bubble butt. They were meaty and hard to my touch. I slapped his ass a few times lightly getting them red and arousing his nerves in that area. Ricky never responded to it. Yep he was flying. I poured more oil across each cheek one and watched as the oil flowed down each one into his crack. I let my palm work across each of those cheeks enjoying the touch of those humpy muscles as they yielded to my hand job. "Guess you've 'never been touched by a guy' butt virginity is gone huh?" I said out loud to my drugged stud, "Well let's just say it's the first of a few virginities that will get lost tonight." I spent some time kneading each meaty cheek savoring the contact then, slowly ran one hand inside the crack. Ricky shuddered slightly as the side of my hand rubbed across his chute. "Still okay sir?" I inquired.

"AAHH," he moaned as I rubbed back and forth across his asshole with the side of my palm. He took a sharp intake of breathe but lay still. I continued my motions across that hole as my macho boxing cop slowly spread his legs to give me greater access. Stud boy liked getting his hole massaged. He spread his powerful tights apart with every new stroke until his butt opening was fully exposed to view. It was pink, moist, and good enough to eat but that might be another time. I grabbed another bottle and applied a different oil on his entryway (this had been laced with a sexual stimulant provided by my cooperative doctor - okay Brent outdid himself that day) and slowly ran my thumb along its ringed muscles. Ricky's breathing intensified as I played with his rim while the stimulant took effect. By now, his chute hole would be tingling with erotic pleasure.

"AAHH," he hissed as his body quaked under my hole massage. Suddenly, his waist rose slightly up as if to accommodate something under it. I tilted my head to see. My cop jock was throwing a boner! He was turned on by the job I was performing on his cherry chute. No doubt about it. I went for broke and inserted a well-oiled finger up Mr. Macho's hole. I wanted him just a bit looser for my next move

"Fuck," he whimpered as my greasy finger entered. "Oh fuck."

I withdrew my finger then took the bottle's nozzle and slipped it into his hole and squeezed. The laced stimulant squirted up deep inside his warm cavern. I wanted to coat his inner lining and hopefully his prostate with the stimulant. I pulled out the bottle and watched as a few drops of oil leaked from his butt hole. I spread his limp legs further apart and began to finger fuck my macho hunk. Ricky groaned as I gave him his first taste of being screwed. He started grinding his crotch into the table. He was feeling the drugs effects in his guts now. I continued pistoning in and out of his chute making sure to hit his prostate every time.

"Fuck, fuck, fuck, fuck." Ricky was now babbling as he began to hump the table.

Yeah baby my thoughts precisely. Time for some reprogramming. I looked at the overhead camera and nodded. Enrico entered from a side door.

"Well Rico, I'd say big brother is primed for some inner brain massage," I laughed as I continued finger fucking his squirming brother. By now Ricky was wiggling his butt, grinding his waist as he humped the table, and moaning sexily.

"Oohhhhaaarrgghh... deeper...futhkin... aahhh," our cop older brother confirmed.

"Who would have thought," grinned Enrico as he watched the scene. "That my super straight stud cop brother would finally get 'busted' himself!"

"And from the fucking he's giving the table he likes it," I replied as I increased my finger screw job on our soon to be transformed jock cop.

"Hey Mickey likes it! He likes it!" Enrico hooted in a parody of a cereal commercial. The room filled with our laughter and Ricky's moans. Time for phase two!

Part Two:
And it's a TKO!

Enrico quickly wiped off our prone stud making sure that the outer hypnotic oils on him were gone (hey no need to get zapped ourselves right) while I continued my finger massage on Ricky's inner charms. Once that was done, we were ready for phase two. I pulled my finger from Ricky's hole and was rewarded by a soft sigh of regret from my cop boxer. Well soon, baby I thought as I patted his bubble butt and walked to the front of the table. We had set up a small strobe light in front of Ricky. Enrico turned it on and I positioned Ricky's head to face it.

"Ricardo, wake up bro." I softly stated. Ricky's eyes fluttered open but from the diluted pupils that stared out this jock was still under the effects of the drug. "Look at the light bro."

Ricky gazed into the lights. "Look Ricky," I said in a firm voice, "look at the lights and go deep inside them." The drug probably made the light show unnecessary but, what the hell; I'm an old-fashioned family values type of guy.

"Deep... looking deep...I 'm so deep... falling," he responded his vision firmly fixed on the flickering lights in front of them

"That's alright Ricky your younger brother will catch you." I assured him. "Your little brother will keep you safe."

"Rico... safe... he keeps me safe," sighed Ricky as he drifted into the next stage. Now for a few well chosen actions and commands.

"Yes," I confirmed to my zonked jock hunk, "Rico will protect you." I signaled to Enrico to get ready. The young Latino picked up the bottle of stimulant oil and gently reinserted it's nozzle into his older stud brother's chute. We had taken time to slightly heat the oil to maximize the feeling for Ricky. Okay we are too kind.

"Rico also brings you pleasure Ricky," I instructed as I nodded to Enrico. The younger brother squeezed the heated oil flooding up inside his older brother's ass.

"Ohh fuccc," Ricky gasped as his guts, still sensitized by the prior oil's stimulation, felt an even more arousing effect as the warm fluid filled his inner chute linings, and washed over his prostate coating the nerves and putting them on heightened sexual vulnerability.

"Feels good inside you right Ricky?" I queried knowing the answer.

"Oh yeahhhh Ricoo... yeaaahhhh," Ricky groaned as his hips once more adjusted on the table. Another boner for Mr. Macho cop. "More... more," he pleaded as his butt lifted slightly in an attempt to press up against the bottle. Close now. Very close. Time for the final round on our boxer. Get ready Ricardo I chuckled to myself. Your machismo straight psyche is about to go down for the count!

"You like that inside you Ricky," I suggested firmly.

"Like... in me," Ricky accepted. His brain was jelly what with the drugs in his system and those flickering lights his eyes were focused on.

"You like it in you. Want more in you." I stated.

"So much. More in my hole. Feels hot and warm." He gasped as Enrico gave a final squirt up big brothers now slicked guts. Enrico inserted a gloved finger in his brother's rectum and began to screw Ricardo.

"Oh...goddd," chattered Ricky as his enflamed inner lining and prostate got another massage. My delirious boxer hunk started to fuck the table under him. I reached under, grabbed his erect uncut 9" Latin meat, and started to jerk him off.

"Feel how good it is getting fucked man." I replied as Enrico and I sexually stimulated our straight boy reprogramming his brain to turn onto male sex.

"Ooowwhhh... Rrriiiiiccoo," our young hunk agreed as he began bucking his hips up and down on the table.

"You want Rico inside you man." I hissed sharply. "You want him in you so bad. He fills up; satisfies that need you have."

"Oh fuc yeah Rico," howled Ricky as he began to gyrate even more on the table responding quite nicely to the sexual manipulations we were doing on his humpy stud body. Loved seeing his butt rising and falling in a fucking motion. In sexual action, that bastard was a hot sight to behold. "Rico in me."

He was ready. Enrico pulled the bottle from Ricky's hole and slipped on a condom to avoid getting infected with the oil inside big brother. He slipped one arm under Ricky's waist lifting Ricardo up onto his knees and straddled between his brother's muscular thighs. Ricky resembled a pyramid now with his shoulders on the table and his ass as the apex. Fucking scorcher of a view guys! Final round boxer boy.

Get ready to hit the canvas!

I continued stroking Ricky's meat, which, now that his lower half was up, looked quite impressive. Thick, long, and thrusting up from a nice dark patch of pubic hair I envied the ladies that had been the recipient of its favors and felt a slight pang of guilt for the future ones that would be left in ignorance. Yeah right!

"Tell Rico what you want boy," I commanded.

"Fuck... in me... Need in me." Ricky babbled almost incoherently.

"YEAH!" hooted Enrico as he drove his cock into his brother. He was finally getting his revenge for all those taunts from Ricky. "Take it bro!"

"AAAAHHHHH FFFUUCC...YYEEAAAHHHH," shouted Ricky as his cherry got popped. Enrico started to fuck now in earnest. At one point, he began to slap his brothers' ass.

SLAP

SLAP

SLAP

"Take it you bastard," he yelled as he fucked his big brother sweet ass and bitch slapped Ricky's cheeks with each drive until they were crimson.

"OOOO...OOOOO...OOOO," Ricky screamed as he got plowed and slapped.

I continued my jerk off on the boy's engorged meat as I shouted my final reconditioning into Ricky's vulnerable pliable inner brain. "You love getting fucked. You love getting fucked. It's hotter than you ever thought. You love cock. You need cock."

Ricky moaned louder. "Oooo...love cock...love cock...hottest sex... needs cock." He began to buck under Enrico and one of his hands reached down to grab his cock from me and masturbate himself. The dude was really into it now. One more thing.

I walked to the front to face Ricky. His eyes shone with pure lust. I dropped my pants and brought my hard cock right up to his mouth. "Ricky loves to taste this. Ricky needs to suck this. It makes that sexual heat he is feeling even hotter," I chanted as Enrico, now ablaze in his glory rammed his brother's ass harder. I noticed that Ricky had also increased the rhyme of his cock massage as well. The zapped cop gazed at my cock in a new light. He began to saliva and then, oh yeah the dude opened his mouth and stuck out his tongue. He was cock hungry!

I slipped my shaft across his wet tongue and guided it in. In a second I felt his warm moist mouth begin to suck away just like a newborn suckling on his mother's tit for nourishment. Enrico raised his hand and we gave each other a high five as we both plowed the former 'don't touch my ass' or 'only pussy takes it up the ass' macho big brother of his with a searing double ended fuck!

"Yeah baby," we both, growled as Ricky grunted in pure pleasure. "You love it. You love it. You will always want it. You can't fight this need anymore!" We roared.

"UUUUUMMMPPPHH," our boxer agreed as he thrust his hips up to meet his little brother's strokes, deepened his blowjob on me, and quickened his hand job on himself. We were all at the edge.

Ricardo suddenly let out a loud muffled guttural groan that came from deep inside him. "AAAAAAAAAAAAA," his cock erupted flooding the table with his hot seed. Enrico and I exploded at once filling boxer boy from both ends. Ricardo, to my surprise, sucked down every bit of my jis.

We had taken on his mind in the ring of sexual desire and had scored a knockout win.

We both got off the table and Ricky slumped back down. From the look of him, he had thoroughly enjoyed his boxing match. Seeing him lying there with some of my jis in the corners of his mouth and panting on the table made it all worthwhile. He was totally mind fucked and was ready for his final training now. I bent in close and began my reprogramming. "Ricky from now on when you hear Enrico say 'Ricardo', your asshole will remember how turned on it was before and it will burn to be fucked. Got it"

"My name, Enrico saying it, need fucking," Ricky replied as his zapped mind drank in the recircuiting.

"You will be overwhelmed by this sexual desire. You will do anything to satisfy it." I stated. You hear him say that name and you need to be fucked badly."

"Need to be fucked. Need to be fucked." Ricky agreed. "Can't fight it."

"You'll also remember how great sucking cock was too," I instructed to his still receptive brain center. "You love sucking cock. You need to suck cock!"

"Love cock, want cock, need suck cock," Ricky repeated as the desire cemented forever onto his inner brain.

"Enrico say the word," I said.

"Ricardo." Enrico whispered.

The effect was electric. Ricky began to groan and tighten his butt cheeks. "My ass...oh my ass." He gasped as his tongue wet his lips indicating that his brain had registered it all. I nodded to a grinning Enrico.

"Okay Ricky sleep now. But keep repeating inside your head what I just told you; remember how great getting fucked felt and how delicious cock tastes," I commanded. Ricky drifted off. We stood there looking at our new to be born cockboy. He had a beautiful grin lying there licking his lips grinding his hips into the table. Well, Ricky I thought, dream on cause soon your new life begins.

"Well Enrico, lets get big brother ready for graduation I smirked as we began to get everything ready. Call Eric and tell him we need him. Hey we got a movie to shoot!"

Part Three:
Officer Down!

Ricky woke up buck naked and tied to a chair. "What the fuck is this?" He roared as he struggled with his bonds. Enrico and I walked into his line of sight. "What the fuck is going on you bastards?" He yelled as he glared first at me then his younger brother. "What the fuck are you doing here Rico?"

"Just came to talk bro," replied Enrico smiling.

"Let me go or I'll beat your ass," an enraged Ricky screamed as his tight sexy body strained against the bindings. He looked even hotter all trussed up but that was a whole different scene.

"Speaking of ass bro," teased Enrico, "tell me, how does yours feel Ricardo?"

"What the fuck about my assss...oh damn," the effect was immediate. Ricky's butt started grinding into his chair.

"Anything wrong Ricardo?" inquired Enrico innocently.

"Oh shit, my ass hole is on fire," said Ricky. The macho cop started squirming in his chair. He was experiencing the first waves of his new sexual needs. Enrico turned to me and nodded. Ricky was going down!

"On fire Ricardo," the younger brother teased. "Feeling funny down there Ricardo?"

Ricky moaned slightly. He kept wiggling in the chair. I noticed that his powerful thighs were now squeezing together, cupping his balls in a viselike grip, and causing his pecker to rise.

"Problem Ricardo?" Enrico continued.

"What the fuck is going on," Ricky groaned as his mind turned on his asshole's need to be fucked and fucked fast. "My ass is so hot."

Enrico leaned in close to Ricky and whispered, "Ricardo what do you want? You can tell me Ricardo."

I could see the sweat beading up on Ricky's face. From the way, he was gyrating in that chair he was turned on big time but from the look in his eyes, he was fighting what his body wanted. Judging by the erection he was sporting and the continual pressure his flexing thighs were inflicting on his ball sack the end to this mental boxing match was a foregone conclusion.

"Tell me Ricardo." The cop's younger brother sneered as he signaled to me to start the video rolling again. I signaled to Eric, who was in the video room throughout all of this, to get it on tape.

"Ricardo tells me. Come on Ricardo what do you want!" Enrico demanded.

Ricky groaned in defeat. "I want someone to fuck me, man," Ricky mumbled as his mind yielded to the sexual need that was consuming it. "Pleasssssseee," he hissed as his body ground into the chair.

"You mean Ricardo you want to take it up the ass like a punta?"

Smirked Enrico as he recalled the smug insults Ricky had thrown about guys taking it up the ass.

"FUCK ME MAN... PLEASE BRO..." Ricky sobbed as his mind spun out of control. "I need a cock up my ass nooooowww." The hypnotic programming was working great.

"Okay bro. But just cause you asked nice." Enrico unzipped and pulled out his meat. "But bro I need you to get my dick slick if it's going to fuck you."

He brought his cock up to Ricky's mouth and waited. His macho older brother stared at the rod that hung so close to his lips. I could see the perspiration on his upper lips. He licked his lips - the dude's mouth was watering! Would he go the distance? "Well Ricardo?"

At the sound of the key word Ricky's newly created sexual needs took over and our straight boy's head instantly bent forward, mouth open, and slobbered over his younger brother's meat. "Oooommmpphhh" was the only sound Ricky made as he worked on his kid brother's manhood.

"That's right, Ricardo," Enrico replied as he gazed at his older brother giving head. "Get it all slick and then I'll fill up that butt of yours. You like the sound of that Ricardo?" He teased.

Ricky must have liked what he heard cause he worked like a pro on that cock. I noticed Mr. Macho cop's own cock leaking up big time in a final confirmation of the transformation we had accomplished. Our one time straight older brother was in full cock slut mode. Enrico untied Ricky's bindings. Ricky, who had not stopped slobbering on his younger brother's cock, slipped off the chair and onto his knees in front of Enrico. He continued blowing his younger brother using one hand to steady himself on Enrico while his other hand reached down to stroke his own engorged dick.

"Si Ricardo. Si Ricardo." Murmured Enrico as he encouraged his older brother's oral service and cemented Ricardo's programming. "Nino bueno, si mi hermano, nino bueno." Enrico encouraged softly as he ran his hand through his older brother's hair and guided him. Ricky moaned and sucked faster. He wanted to be fucked so bad now and would do whenever Enrico wanted him too. Enrico had the key to poor old Ricardo's entrance. I looked at Enrico who was a vision of pure triumph, gave him a thumbs up, then left him to his victory, and hurried home. I was sure he and Eric had the new Dog Bone movie shoot fully in hand.After all, I had my own brother waiting to be serviced.

So there you have it, another arrogant brother on his knees and howling to get screwed by his little brother. Some guys would kick back I guess and enjoy the fruits of their labors but, I had a new movie business to keep up as a going concern. I seem to recall that Eric had mentioned a sexy older brother who was a real arrogant bastard that was currently serving in the marines. Oh well, does the work ever end?

THE PRISONER EXCHANGE

Part One:
Nice Puppy!

"Okay prisoner," the colonel growled at the handcuffed man in front of him. You have three days in the brig for screwing up at usual. He looked at the prisoner in disdain. Before him was a disgrace of a soldier he thought. Small, slight, constantly making mistakes. This man needed to be drummed out, the colonel thought. Well, three days in the brig on base should do the trick! "Sgt.," he buzzed on his intercom, "send in Corporal Shey." the door opened and in walked Shey. At 6' of sculpted muscle and wearing his dark hair, "high and tight" Corporal Shey was the colonel's idea of a marine M.P..

"Corporal Shey." he growled to the M.P. who was at attention, his blue eyes taking in the prisoner with a look of disgust. "This sad excuse for a soldier needs to be guarded. I know the entire base will be deserted for maneuvers in the field but I need you to stay and guard him. Will you need help?"

"Help with him," snorted the corporal. "Not a problem at all sir!" The colonel smiled, yes, this was the answer he expected of his best M.P. Corporal Shey was as gung ho macho a marine as they came. All man and filled with "semper fi." He kicked butt on the base. Yes, he could do it.

"Good then. Prisoner is yours corporal. I'm off."

The corporal took the prisoner to the barracks. He roughly pushed the cuffed man into the cell. "Turn around asshole," he barked, "If you try anything funny as I take off your cuffs I'll pound your sorry wimp ass into the ground." Yeah, he thought, this guy a problem? Not for this hotshot M.P.! Shey reattached the cuffs to the front of the prisoner. He sneered at the man. A true piece of crap he thought! The prisoner reached up and started rubbing his eyes.

"NOW WHAT!" yelled Shey.

"I think a cinder got in my eye sir," the prisoner moaned, "please sir can you see if it's there?"

"Shit...oh all right where let me see," Shey gazed into the prisoners eyes, "nothing there," he grumbled.

"No there is look deeper sir," the prisoner whispered so softly that Shey had to concentrate to hear him.

"Nothing," Shey replied his eyes feeling funny as he concentrated on the prisoners pupils. The guy's pupils seemed to pull Shey in and he found himself blinking repeatedly. "Deeper...deeper...look deeper." the prisoner rthymically stated in tones that seemed to come from far away.

"Nothinnthin...I...I...doooonn't..." murmured Shey feeling sleepy and light headed.

"You see it...look deep...feel it...you're sleepy and relaxing now." the prisoner's voice filling the corporal's head.

"I...don't...thseee...a...thin...sooo sleeeppyyyy." Replied a yawning Shey, his body weaving, those muscular arms now hanging loose at his sides. Shey's eyelids began to droop. A small voice in him seemed to tell him not to look anymore but then, it faded, as he felt all warm and fuzzy. A silly grin broke out on Shey's face.

"That's right," smiled the prisoner as he reached over to take the keys to his cuffs from the dazed corporal's belt. "Night, night stud OK."

"Slleeepppyyyy thir...goood...nniiiitteee," Shey moaned as he drifted off.

The prisoner looked at his hypnotized guard. Big macho stud, he thought. Colonel's pride boy. An idea struck him! "Strip boy!" The M.P. obeyed at once. The prisoner watched as his 'guard peeled out of his M.P. uniform. "Slower boy," he commanded. "Like you were in a strip joint!" Shey complied and the prisoner was treated to a great show as the M.P. erotically pulled off his clothes in a sensual and suggestive tease that was highly erotic!

The prisoner inspected the bare marine stud in front of him gazing at his muscled torso with its hard six-pack. He walked up to the sleeping M.P. and fondled his 9"uncut cock and hefty balls–a deep sigh came from the hypnotized marine and his rod began to stiffen. "Like that boy," he inquired.

"Yesssss," Shey replied while the prisoner rolled the M.P.'s impressive bull sack in his hands. The response was noted by the prisoner.

The prisoner then sauntered behind the "captive" and massaged the M.P.'s bubble butt. Nice firm melons he thought. Slipping a finger between the cheeks, he tickled the M.P.'s chute causing the once macho stud to squirm and groan even more in pleasure. Shey's grin grew in size while his marine meat filled out even further!

"New feeling there boy," snickered the prisoner as he tickled the ring of his 'captive.

"Ohh...fuckkkk," a squirming Shey responded.

"Ever been fucked boy." asked the man as he watched Shey groan and try to back up onto the probing finger.

"Noooo...ooohhh..." Shey said as he succeeded in pushing the man's finger past the outer ring muscles! "AAHHH..." the M.P. gasped as a wider grin came to his handsome face

The prisoner stopped and removed his finger from Shey's hole causing the hunky M.P. to moan in disappointment. Perhaps the macho M.P. was latent the man thought. That would explain the over exaggerated macho marine demeanor. He walked back to face his former guard. A smile came over him. A little lesson for the colonel and his "pet" marine was in the future! Hell, he might even be doing good old Shey a favor by bringing his true nature out! Quickly the prisoner got out of his prisoner jumpsuit and redressed in the M.P.'s uniform.

Handing his 'former' guard the jumpsuit he ordered, "Open your eyes butthead. Get dressed now, you hear me asswipe!" Shey quickly responded.

The 'M.P.' went up to his prisoner and stared at the former M.P.'s unfocused pupils, "now listen carefully" he whispered to Shey, "your a prisoner whose a general fuck up you got it," Shey nodded dully.

"General fuck up..." he mumbled.

"Yeah," laughed the M.P. at Shey, "and you hate that don't you because you're a pansy, pussy right."

"Hate that," Shey repeated as his eyes filed with tears at the shame of it all, "cause I'm a pansy, pussy." The M.P. hooted in pleasure. He had this arrogant stud in the palm of his hand!

"But, I'm your M.P. who is going to make you better." He sneered.

"Better yes sir," Shey replied as a dumb smile broke out on his face.

"That's right son," said the M.P., "but maybe you don't deserve it. Maybe if you beg though I'll do it."

"Oh please sir," moaned Shey dropping down on his knees before his M.P. savior, "I'm a total asswipe pansy, pussy who needs your help"!

As he stared at the groveling former M.P. - now prisoner - the man chuckled." Ok asshole. But you must obey me at all times."

"Yes sir," replied a joyful tear stained Shey.

The man pulled Shey to his feet and glared into the hypnotized mans eyes." Big macho M.P. huh. I'm no problem for the colonel's pet right!" He snarled as Sheys eyes widened. "I've seen you walking around like a two bit god. Showing off in the gym, on maneuvers, busting the lowly private grunts as you call them. Who is the one in control now bastard?"

"You, sir," nodded the flying former M.P.," please sir, change me from a fuck up piece of crap sir"

The new M.P. laughed. "Well then, time for some dog training! By the way fucker," the man snorted as he led his 'trainee' to the showers while remembering how nice Shey's butt felt, "did I tell you my favorite pooch is a Mexican hairless..."

Three days later the colonel returned from maneuvers to find his "pet M.P." totally naked on all fours wearing a studded dog collar, shaved bare of all body hair, barking like a dog with his tongue hanging out and, performing "tricks" to the hoots of the assembled soldiers. The grunts were having a field day, finally able to get back at the M.P. who had busted their chops in the past while holding them up to ridicule. Some of them had video recorders going, getting all of it on tape others just cameras! Revenge was sweet!

"Hey doggie," one chubby soldier commanded to the marine 'dog' as his squad chuckled, "want a treat boy. Got one for you." The pudgy soldier held out a candy bar. Shey padded up to the grunt on all fours then assumed a begging position, his arms at his sides and tongue hanging out, staring at the soldier with a devoted look.

"Arf. Arf." he barked waiving his ass and keeping his mouth open as the assembled soldiers cracked up in pleasure. The fat soldier winked at his friends remembering how Shey had taunted him in front of these same men many times before. Now it was his turn. "Roll over then boy," he ordered. "Then you get the treat." Shey instantly rolled onto his back, his legs and arms bent close to his body.

"Good boy," sneered the soldier as he threw the 'dog' the candy bar. Shey snapped it up and barked louder returning to a kneeling position on all fours.

"Shey," stated another soldier who had also been abused by

the M.P. in the past, "I think you should mark your territory boy, don't you?"

Shey lumbered over to the flagpole and to the delighted hoots of the amazed soldiers, he lifted his left leg and urinated on the pole. The soldiers went crazy as they snapped pictures and taped the entire scene. Shey, his eyes in a hypno daze just smiled and barked in delirious joy.

Then, just as they thought, it couldn't get any better Shey, still on all fours, lifted his right leg, bent at his waist and, began to lick himself clean! That story alone would be repeated often throughout the service in the future. By now, everyone was in the spirit of the fun!

"Roll over. Roll over." The troops chanted to their newest mascot. Shey ever the obedient canine (and, thanks to a permanent deep hypnotic reprogramming that defied the marine corps best hypno experts who tried in vain to cancel it, Shey would become a canine for three days every month without warning – a few times the soldiers would parade their 'pup' during visitors day despite all efforts by the brass to stop it) flipped on his back and rolled on the muddy field! As he did, he growled in sheer delight his flaccid cock slapping his muscled abs!

As the colonel stared in horror at the sight of his prized marine, groveling in the dirt for the men's amusement his eyes caught sight of Shey's newly shaved butt. The image he saw on Shey's bare ass turned the colonel weak. There, for all the world to see was a newly inscribed tattoo big as life saying just simply "semper fido"!

On a nearby rooftop, the former prisoner watched the results of his work in glee. His eyes strayed over to take in the colonel. Hmmm, not a bad looking man he thought. Built in a lean muscular way, at 44 still distinguished but young, handsome, a totally macho gung ho marine, highly arrogant and, from his reputation, a real ladies man. Yep, a prize worth taking the former prisoner decided. Besides, he promised Shey a playmate he chuckled to himself!

Part Two:
Colonel Canine

It had been a rough month for Colonel Barry, his best marine M.P. reduced to a dog by a prisoner who was still on the loose. He sat in his office drained. The general expected the "mess," as he called it to be cleaned up fast. Barry looked at himself in the nearby mirror. He liked what he saw. At 44, he was still young for his rank with a lean tight muscular body, just a hint of grey in his brown hair and clear blue eyes. A gung ho marine since 18 he prided himself on his manhood, physical ability and, cut no slack for anyone less than all man in his book. As he saw it, a marine was macho, hard drinking, and took women at his whim. He would not fail. No, that escaped prisoner was no match for him! As he pondered, his next move there was a knock at his door.

"Come in," he growled. The door opened to reveal a cleaning man.

"Sorry sir," the man said in a shaky voice, "I did not know you were working late."

The colonel frowned at the man barely noticing him. What a loser he thought as a smile came to his lips. "Well, get on with it then," he sneered.

The man pulled out a rag, "I'll just dust fast sir," he said quietly, "let me just shake it clean first." With that, the man shook the dirty rag right in the colonel's face causing dust to fly directly into Barry's eyes.

"YOU IDIOT!" Barry sputtered trying to get the dust out of his now burning eyes.

"Oh sir". Moaned the man, "please sir, let me help clean it.

"Stay away from me you sad excuse for a man," yelled the colonel.

"Sir, that was pretty grainy dust I better check your eyes, sir. Don't want to cause an infection from anything still there!" uttered the cleaning man.

"Oh, all right," Barry answered quickly. What next he thought!

"Open wide colonel," the man stated in a calm steady voice. "Look directly into my eyes so I can check."

The colonel stared into the man's eyes. "See anything, he asked?" The mans pupils seemed to grow filling his entire vision.

"Not sure sir," the man whispered softly "look deeper."

"Deeper," muttered the colonel who felt as if he was falling into those warm dark spots in front of him. "Look deeper," he sighed as he felt a waive of calm come over him.

"Almost done," said the cleaning man as he noticed with approval the colonel's eyelids starting to droop. "Give it up now; fall in; I'll catch you."

"Catch me," sighed the colonel,"give it up, yes!"

"Yes sir, boy," laughed the man.

"Sir!" responded the colonel who felt so tired that he began to yawn.

"Tired huh," whispered the man firmly.

"Very sirth," Barry slurred barely able to stay awake.

"Then sleep boy," ordered the man.

"Thsleeeeep, sthir." A feeling of well being swept over Barry as he drifted off. He was so sleepy and he liked the nice man for letting him rest. Yes, he thought as darkness feel across his mind. He was a nice man!

The cleaning man laughed as he stared at the unconscious figure swaying in front of him. Got you, asshole, he stated out loud. Too bad, he pondered that the colonel never bothered to really look at him. After all, he probably never expected that his wanted 'prisoner' was going to come right to him!

"Okay colonel," he said as he began to strip the officer of his clothes, "time to go through some new basic training!"

He looked over his prize. Not bad, he thought as he ran his hands over the colonels pec, nipples, and abs. Yep, quite nice especially that bubble butt. That cherry will be well worth the picking tonight. But first, the man chuckled; let's have a bit of fun right now. As the man recalled Barry was always bragging about his manhood and the endurance of his 'helmeted warrior' in action. Hmmm lets start there he decided. He whispered something in Barry's ear then stepped back

"Open those eyes asshole," he barked. Barry's eyes popped open but from the hazy look in them, it was obvious that Barry was out of it big time!

"Now boy, think you're a hot babe stud huh," the man growled.

A smiled flickered across Barry's face, "Yes sir!" he stated. "Wrong pussyboy!" the man replied as he grabbed the colonel's 9" uncut cock. "This is a boy's equipment! Hell, I bet you can't even get a hardon boy." The man released his grip.

"I can, sir, "insisted Barry.

"Show me," smiled the man in eager anticipation. Barry took his meat firmly in hand and began a steady stroke but despite some darkening, the cock remained totally flaccid!

"Problem son," inquired the man in a voice dripping in false concern.

"I can't... It won't..." Sputtered Barry as he redoubled his efforts. The room filled with the sounds of Barry's rapid breathing and the slapping of flesh against flesh. Despite all his efforts, though Barry's cock remained soft! He looked up at the man in shock and embarrassment unaware that the man had 'fixed' Barry's mind with a hypnotic order to remain unaroused!

Now listen up and repeat after me. "I'm a punk kid whose screwed up bad," the man laughed as he took Barry's former 'helmeted warrior' firmly in hand.

Barry looked down at his rod, which seemed to shrink before his eyes in the man's hands. It was true he thought and his eyes filled with tears. "Yes sir," he whined in a cracking voice. "Screwed up punk kid sir!" responded Barry sounding even more like a pre pubescent kid.

Oh, this will be great thought the man, this macho marine is super susceptible to suggestions! "Matter of fact it doesn't even deserve to have this hair around it does it!" the man said coolly.

"No sir," retorted Barry the shame reflected in the tears streaming down his cheeks, "I'm just a punk kid sir. I don't deserve man hairs sir!"

"Well, punk I will take care of that all right." laughed the man.

A huge grin came to Barry's face, "thank you sir!"

The man reached into his pants and pulled out his cock. Tell you what boy. I'll let you taste a real man just this once all right. You love cock boy remember," he repeated in a whisper.

Barry glanced into the man's eyes intensely drifting away once more into that peaceful acceptance. "Love man cock, yes sir." Barry replied to the suggestion eagerly. The former straight stud gazed in awe at the man's meat. In a second, he was on his knees sucking away in pure delight.

"Do it right, boy," the man stated as he signaled Barry to look in his eyes again. Barry locked his eyes on the man as ordered. Now stare deep boy in my eyes while you suck... After you are done you will drift off to sleep till I clap my hands then, you will awake thinking you are a nice doggie. Got it, Barry moaned his agreement as he sucked that tasty meat. Even as he worked on that delicious cock a part of him felt like a pooch and, in the recesses of his mind, he heard himself barking already. The man ran his hands along Barry's neck and he felt a nice leather dog collar being attached by the man. Yes, the man thought, as he got ready to fill the colonel up with his juice, this should be quite a nice training session, but first, there was a M.P. canine to pick up on the base named Shey. Heck, why not make it a double fun night the man thought as he remembered the tight butt hole of his first conquest, good old Corporal Shey!

Days later as the general was at his desk a pale orderly came in.

"What do you want Lt.," the general growled.

"Sir, outside," the Lt. stated in a quivering voice. "It's happened again." "What!" yelled the general in annoyance.

"You better see, sir," replied the Lt..

The general got up and looked out his window. There in plain sight in front of the wives club with all the officer's wives looking on were Barry and Shey completely naked! They were on all fours wearing dog collars and... dear GOD they were sniffing each other's butts in broad daylight with their cocks semi hard. As they stuck their noses into each other's asses, the women laughed in high humor. Quite a few of the women had been screwed by either man then dumped - this was fantastic! The general ran out to the scene just in time to see Shey try to 'mount' a whimpering colonel Barry! He was in total shock. As he approached all he could hear was the two officers barking their heads off in total abandon. Finally, he arrived at the two 'canines' and pulled them apart, he stood between them while a disappointed Barry and Shey sniffed his legs. The women tittered in glee. The general glared at the amused women. "Ladies," he growled, "this is hardly a source of amusement..." but he then felt something wet and warm hitting both his legs. He looked down in rage to discover that both Barry and Shey had 'marked' each of his legs with their urine. The women erupted in applause as the furious general stared helpless at his predicament. Unaware of it all, Barry and Shey frolicked around the soaked general yelping in joy!

FROM TOP TO BOTTOM

The name is Miguel. I work out of a club in midtown. You know the type of place one of those sleazy hustler places filled with two types: Latino or black rough trade and the white rich businessmen who want to take a walk in the hood.

Well, I do fine there. My stats: 5' 9", 175lbs of gym toned muscle complete with six pack, 31 inch waist, 9" rod, and light honey color hair. My rules are simple: sex safe, ass no way, pay up front, and top service only! I work when I want, with whomever I want, no cut to the owner but hell, for the prices, he charges on the shit he says is booze he makes out okay. Besides, I'm the hottest stud he's got here so, he puts up with it–I draw them in.

It was a slow night the day I saw him come in. Short Asian guy, I'd say about 5'6", built though and not bad looking either. I noticed him talking to the owner and looking in my direction out of the corner of my eye. They shook hands like they were old friends and then he walked over to me.

"The man over there says your name is Miguel," he stated in a voice that hinted at his arousal.

I turned to face him sizing him up – not bad clothes, should get a good price out of him for my work. It was then that I saw his medallion a golden dragon with two eyes that sparkled with two stones I couldn't quite make out. He saw me staring at it.

"Ah yes, the dragon of power," he whispered, "it rules men's inner souls."

"Yeah, whatever man," I stated, "look you see anything you want here? If so, it costs okay."

"Yes I want." he laughed, "very much so."

"Good," I replied, "then let's get it right out front. I'm no bottom, its safe, or nothing, and I don't kiss guys. You pay up front $300 per hour, we clear."

"Very, but can we stay for a drink first," he asked as he signaled the owner. In a flash, the man was directing us to a back table and serving us himself. Hmm, I thought, this guy must rate high and I figured perhaps that I should have doubled the fee. I tasted my drink - hey, this was the good stuff! The guy must have noticed my surprise.

"Yes, the owner knows that my tastes are good," he spoke in a voice that almost purred. "His usual fare is not for me - but, drink up Miguel."

Well, it was his wallet so I drank the first and ordered a double. As I drank I noticed that the lights in the bar where causing the stones in his medallion to sparkle. He saw me staring at it again and laughed.

"Yes, the dragon's eyes do catch the light. If you stare, deeply enough you will find that in the center there is a small dragon in each stone. Look yourself."

I looked at them, they did flicker in the light... but a dragon, come on man! "Sorry, I don't see it," I replied.

"You must gaze deeper Miguel," he responded in a quiet steady voice.

Well, I figure, the liquor is good and what the fuck it's his money I'm getting. So I figure I'd play along. I look!

"I think I see something," I reply barely concealing my smirk.

"Yes, but it must be seen by looking deeper," he said.

I stare at the center and after a few minutes, it hits me. I think I do see it! "Hey, man," I state, kinda surprised now, "It's there! A fucking dragon I think!"

That's right...you will see it clearer if you look deeper. See it clearer yet, look deeper now." The light flickered in the eyes; I found I couldn't gaze away!

"What... do...what..." I had a bit of difficulty answering for some reason now.

"Deeper." He whispered.

I tried to look away. I couldn't. Those flickering lights–drawing me in! I could see - a freaking dragon coming out of the depths.

"Deeper." He ordered.

No way, a voice, now fading fast, yelled inside me. Get away from that thing! I felt a cold sweat breaking out but I couldn't move! I couldn't stop staring. It was like I was falling toward that dragon with only his steady voice to hold onto. I felt my eyes widen and heard only his voice.

"Almost there Miguel." He laughed.

Some part of me was screaming that I had to stop. Hell, I was the top guy in this business deal. I fucking called the shots! But, it was no use, my mind's resistance started to collapse as his voice filled every corner of my brain. A huge dragon appeared before me reaching out to devour me. I just stayed there helpless till it fucking engulfed me in its claws!

"Almost...ah yes, you are there!" he laughed, the only sound I could now hear. "Look at me Miguel," he ordered! I raised my head; it felt like I was in some dream.

"You will go into the back room and strip then, stand at attention legs spread, hands behind your head. Understand!"

I felt powerless to resist "yes," I replied groggily.

"That is yes master," he growled.

"Yes, master," I answered to my amazement. Then I got up, went into the backroom, stripped, braced my hands behind my head, and waited!

After what seemed like an hour, he entered. He walked around me inspecting me from every angle. Finally, he spoke. "Hypnosis is a good tool. The subject loses his will to the master. Of course, a little liquor weakens even the best will wouldn't you say Miguel." He laughed as my stomach knotted. "So you are 'el hombre' I hear. Hmm perhaps we should change that," he walked to a table and picked up a pair of scissors. I stared in fear. He saw my eyes and laughed softly shaking his head. "No, no not that, just a little return to childhood!" He walked up to me took my cock in his hands and started to trim my crotch hairs. I stared down in shock unable to move. HE WAS REMOVING MY MAN HAIRS! He stared at my face and laughed.

"That's right Miguel; see it slowly falling away with each hair. Your manhood is going in each cut."

I stared as he cut my manhood away. Watching as each hair floated to the floor like a gentle snow with each cut. I felt weaker with each snip!

"Going."

I cringed as the floor filled with a shower of my Latin hairs. A part of me howled in shame and protest but my voice remained silent!

"Going."

Oh, no I screamed in my mind. Don't turn me into a punk kid! I was getting younger. More submissive.

"Almost gone, feel it!"

He was right; I could sense the man in me fading away, my man's inner voice growing fainter and fainter. I was becoming a child in his hands. The macho stud image I always had was barely clinging on now!

He stopped and walked to the table. I watched in horror as he returned with shaving cream and a razor. He foamed my crotch and balls and started to scrape away my man stubble.

Scrape.

Madre de dios, he was unmanning me forever!

Scrape.

NO, I was "el hombre," not some bare crotched pussy!

Scrape.

I watched in horror as he cleaned my manhood away. It was no use, I was demanded! My image fell off the cliff into a deep pit! Soon I was hairless but he wasn't done yet because he foamed my pits and cleaned them off. Then my legs and chest! The cold air hit my shaved body but I couldn't move. When he was finished, he brought a mirror for me to see the result. I was bare of all the hair I grew when I became a man.

"Ah, now you are returned to whom you really are," he whispered, "not Miguel the hot Latin top but Miguelito a young bottom!"

I stared at him in shock but he just smiled and rubbed my cheek. "Tonight you will learn, through hypnosis many things Miguelito. How to prolong pleasure and pain, how sensitive your ass is, and how to surrender all will to another. It will take time, child, but you are under my control and everyday that hypnotic control will be strengthened till one day you will be completely content to offer your ass to everyone."

I just stood there and gazed at him. He had my Latin ass in his pocket. Tears began to fill my eyes, as they rolled off my cheek; he reached over to touch them.

"Ah, the loss of your manhood continues Miguelito, very good. Here, lick the moisture from my fingertips!"

He extended his fingers and I licked - sucking on them like a baby sucks its mother's tit – bitter salt filled my mouth. This former hot Latin stud was now bawling and sucking like a baby! I felt weak and powerless to fight him. Hell, a new image was rapidly filling in the void by the second one. Miguelito the boy was being borne! It only needed one last push to imprint it all in me permanently and, that was about to be done.

"I am now going to introduce you to 'milking' my Miguelito; and, for that we need help." He clapped his hands and the door opened - the club owner entered!

"Bill, I want to milk Miguelito but I need you to heat him up for me. So you fuck him while I pump his Latin cock of its prime juices!"

I stared in silent protest but it did no good. Bob stripped and came behind me. I felt his cock press against my Latin cherry hole.

"Miguel," the master said, "relax your hole so Bob can enter."

I tried to protest but, even as my mind rebelled, I could feel my ass muscles relax and open. Bob must have felt it too because he pushed in me in one thrust. I gasped – the first sound I had made thus far. When I did, they both laughed!

"That's right, Bob, fuck the boy hard and good. See, he must like it, his dick is hard."

I gazed down – IT WAS TRUE! MY HEAD STARTED TO SPIN. HOW COULD THIS BE!

As I tried to grasp this all the master took my rod in one of his hands and started to jerk me off into a cup that his other hand was holding! Soon, I was moaning under the two-sided assault.

"That's right Miguelito," cooed the master as he pumped my meat faster, "give into it boy and shoot your hot Latin spunk into this cup I have. My clientele will pay top dollar for your jism and I intend to 'milk' you until all my orders are filled!"

A part of me wanted to refuse but that part got fainter and fainter till all I felt was his hand and Bob's dick ramming open my virgin butt. My asshole was firing intense pleasure throughout my body by now. I finally gave into it all and the next thing I knew I was shooting gallons of my juices into the master's cup.

"Good boy," said the master as Bob pulled out of me. He came up close and bent forward. I felt his lips on mine and the next thing I realize I was deep throating him. I explored his inner mouth like a thirsty boy needing a drink bad. My brain was spinning out of control needing the taste of his lips badly! He pulled away and smirked. "Not bad...but you will learn over time, right?" I just fucking nodded. The master then went to the table and came back with another cup!

"Bob, send in some of your studs. I need to get this order finished and I'll need a few more fresh cocks screwing 'Miguelito ' tonight so his pump stays primed! I anticipate about four hours of 'milking' so send in one every fifteen minutes over the next four hours!"

I looked at their smiling faces and then at my bare body. I was theirs from now on, a fucking jism factory to be used like a piece of crap. It was no use, his mind control was too strong, and, after tonight, my Latin top days were be over!

Well, it's been a long year of daily hypnotic control and suggestion. My old reputation is long forgotten now and some new stud has filled the gap I suppose. I've been the master's best milking cow for him and his clientele. Yeah, many changes. Wish I had time to fill you on every detail but the master has sent for me. Seems there is to be a new 'milking' session for a few friends! My master needs his prized heifer'. So, what can I say but...

MOOOOOOOO!

ABOUT THE AUTHOR

Kyle Cicero is a native of the NYC metro area. When not thinking up new tales he spends his time discovering novel aspects of gay life in the ever changing city that he calls home. This work is the first in a series of stories that he began on a bet from a friend where he explores the varied areas of erotic male on male sex when coupled with mind control.

www.ingramcontent.com/pod-product-compliance
Lightning Source LLC
Chambersburg PA
CBHW071219260626
47162CB00004B/1361